Richard's Key

A Novel

Sandi Huddleston-Edwards

To Bob,
Live in God's
grace always.
Isaiah 11:6b
Sandi HE

Richard's Key

A Novel

Sandi Huddleston-Edwards

CPCC
PRESS

Central Piedmont Community College

Published by
CPCC Press
PO Box 35009
Charlotte, NC 28235
www.cpccservicescorp.com
cpccpress@cpcc.edu

ISBN: 978-1-59494-019-7
Printed in the United States of America

Cover photo by Ch. Jeremy Cannada
Cover design by Susan Alford

All biblical quotations are from the New Revised Standard Version (NRSV) Bible.

Dedication

It is with humble joy, great praise, and much love that I dedicate this book to my Lord and Saviour, Jesus Christ. To God be all the glory.

And I dedicate this book to Richard. Thank you for your inspirational life of reverence, witness, and love for God and for your faith, hope, and goodness that knew no bounds.

Acknowledgements

It is a privilege to thank the many people who have made this story and book possible. First, I thank my soul mate and dear husband, Barry, whose love and belief in me serve as gentle prods that envelope me with the courage and strength I need to strive for my dreams. Your arms are my safe haven and a place to fall when I'm weary. I love you very much.

Ch. Jeremy Cannada, my father's namesake and my beloved son, because of you I have the most precious title of all— Mother. You continuously amaze me with your intelligence and foresight and make me proud. You are an inspirational Minister of God's Word and Sacrament – something Richard wanted to be when he grew up. Thank you for your creative design, your photographic eye, and your endearing support of my "dream come true."

My undying love and gratitude goes to my precious sister, Teresa George. You are my best friend, my confidant, and my inspiration. I thank God for all of the memories, laughter, and tears that we have shared. You have been my life-long companion, and I can't comprehend a world without your love and support. I tried it for three years until you were born, and it was a lonely time.

To Richard Griffin, my publisher, and Susan Alford, my editor and creative designer: Thank you for taking a chance on a new author and believing in my abilities to bring this story to life through the pages of this book. Because of you, Richard's life and witness have a conduit to touch the lives of many others. You have made this experience surreal and the process painless. You truly have made "my dreams come true." I thank you from the bottom of my heart.

And I'm deeply grateful to those I proudly call "family" and "friend" and who constantly shower me with love, happiness, and sustaining prayers. Their loving encouragement means everything: Tommy Cannada, for walking this walk with me early on and for giving me a beautiful son; Jackie

Huddleston, my mother; Johnny George, my special brother; Ashley and Jonathan George; Laura Avery; Jeff, Jodie, Chase and Chesney Edwards; Todd, Amberly and Railey Edwards; Essie and Jerry Cates; Susan Wood; Bruce Lassiter; Pat and Paul Rigsbee; Robby, Karen, Lindsay, Emily, and Cameron Strombeck; Jeff, Pam, Jared, and Kelsey Gillis; Eddie Edwards; Aaron, E, and Rachel May; Robby, Margaret, Philip, Jennifer, Caite, and Zac Westmoreland; Nathan and Sarah Wells; Peggy Baker; Harriet Keith.

And to Neely-Noel, my Yorkshire Terrier and "baby girl," — you love me unconditionally and are my cherished companion. Thank you for keeping me company as I wrote this book.

Many thanks to my pastors for their profound faith, their heartfelt teachings, and their uplifting prayers for me and my family: Rev. Linda McMillan Bowman; Rev. Phil Hargrove; Rev. Brenda Tapia; Rev. Sheila Council; and Rev. Dr. Malcolm Brownlee.

And my gratitude goes to the many people whose memories and never-ending encouragement assisted me in bringing this novel to fruition: Mack and Helen Wicker; Karen Mather; Pearl McBride; Patrick Payne; Roberta Bowman; Betsy Humphries; Diane Denton; Kenny Harmon; Debra Jones; Mama Sarah Washam; Anne Waddington; Caroline Waddington; Dr. Debra Bosley; Dr. Anita Moss; Dr. Richard B. McKenzie; Jo Ellen Huddleston; Al and JoAnne Huddleston; Bill, Peggy, and Wayne Huddleston; Irene Hewitt; Richard Huddleston; Bonnie Huddleston; Linda S. Parker; Aunt Eunice; Jean Snyder; Kay Saville; Barbara Rawls; Cindy Young; Lori Austin; Bradley Rash; John Shuler; Pat and Dave McCord and Dave's little black rock, and Kenny Harmon.

And finally, my deepest gratitude and love – and humble apologies for my creativity – go to Marvin, Ora, Eugene, Miriam, Vera, Ray, Earl, Richard, Elizabeth Ann, and Ralph. I miss you all.

Prologue

The soul becomes dyed with the color of its thoughts.
Marcus Aurelius

"Isn't this the corner where Mark used to sell newspapers?" the younger brother asked. A wide toothy grin framed his even white teeth contrasted against a suntanned face. He was handsome, and he knew it. The coy glances of admiring multi-aged females confirmed that.

"Yeah," the eldest brother answered casually. He propped his left hand on the supporting post of the red-faced, menacing stop sign at the corner of Front and Market Streets and watched as a young mother scolded her small child. He wasn't sure of the child's sex. A slight frown twisted the corners of his mouth before he slowly turned away from the discipline in progress and squinted his dark brown eyes to silently trace the path of the short cobblestone street to its origin between multi-storied brick buildings. The cobblestones ran one block to the hazy waterfront where a lonely tugboat bellowed loudly, announcing its return to the wooden dock on the other side of the expansive river. He motioned to his brother. "Let's get something to eat."

"Sounds like a winner to me," the younger man replied with a grin.

The two brothers made small talk as they nonchalantly strolled side by side down Front Street. The angry horns of cars and trucks blared loudly, occasionally drowning out their baritone voices and shattering their separate thoughts. The younger brother was taller at 6' 1". His lanky frame shadowed that of his elder brother's who was four inches shorter and weighed within a pound or two of his own weight. Here and there a burst of laughter added to the loud hustle and bustle of the busy street. They slowed their pace, enticed by the aroma of fried seafood, and stopped in front of a restaurant on the corner. Here, they both cupped their hands, shielding their eyes from the afternoon sun's glare, and peered into the finger-smudged window. Displayed on a bed of crushed ice were white filets of flounder, plump gray and pink shrimp, and succulent oysters. The provincial red and white checked curtains outlined the wood-framed window. Peering deeper into the restaurant's interior, the elder brother noticed a distinguished-looking woman sitting at a nearby table facing the window.

Instantly, her eyes met his. He elbowed the ribs of his brother to get his full attention and then nodded politely to the woman. She stopped a full-laden fork in mid-air before primly and properly smiling in his direction. Then she returned her focus to the steaming crab legs and melted butter on the plate before her. Her acknowledgement amused him, so he wasn't quite finished with their non-verbal conversation yet. Knowing that she'd eventually look back, he continued to stare intently in her direction. As he predicted, she did but seemed startled by his impolite and utter disregard for her privacy. Her dinner partner, a bald, portly man with a huge hawk-shaped nose, was oblivious and intently ate his fish. She looked irritatingly in his direction and realized he was missing this unorthodox scene happening right in front of his nose. The eldest brother smirked at the high-rolling businessman in his well-tailored, pin-striped suit.

"What are you doing?" the younger man asked in disbelief. "Are you flirting with that old lady?" His idol was up to something – probably mischief as usual.

"Of course not. I'm just having some fun," the elder brother replied flippantly. He didn't divert his eyes from that of the woman's. "Besides, Gertrude probably hasn't been flirted with in years."

"Gertrude?" He laughed and continued watching the silent exchange.

Assured he had her attention, the elder brother extended his index finger and pointed to the large frozen flounder. Then he pointed to the center of his chest. The lady's silver

eyebrows were raised ambiguously – in indignation and curiosity. Intently, she followed his gestures. Next, he flicked his
left wrist and with his right hand began reeling in an invisible
fish. Finally, he pointed to his chest again and to the large fish.
Their eyes held - his brown and penetrating - hers blue and
steely. She was totally mesmerized by his antics. Eventually,
she broke the strange trance by nodding her head slowly and
smiling. She raised two jewelry-clad hands and clapped daintily as the upper class might do at the opera.

The prankster bowed graciously in acceptance of her
silent applause.

"Roy, you're full of it. You haven't changed a bit."

Roy's chuckling became infectious, and soon his brother was laughing. They laughed so hard their sides hurt. As
the younger brother wiped stray tears from his sky-blue eyes,
they noticed the indignant look the lady gave now. She was
tapping her dinner partner on the arm to get his attention and
was pointing towards the window.

"Come on. Let's get outta here," the younger brother
said as he pulled his mischievous companion's stiff arm. "Well,
we won't be eating seafood. You've taken care of that!"

Still laughing, they turned into a small hamburger
joint with six small booths, a wooden counter, and eight silver stools. The joint had a huge "Drink Coca-Cola®" sign in
the window. Two white-haired men with weathered skin sat
on two of the eight red and chrome spinning stools. They ap-
athetically glanced in the direction of the two younger men
before cramming hamburgers into their wrinkled, waiting
mouths. A matronly lady who wore a white starched apron
and a blue gingham-checked dress approached them as soon
as they sat down.

"You boys look hungry. What can I get for you?" she
asked with a welcoming smile. Her heavily-painted lips were
bright with red lipstick that bled onto her front, yellowing
teeth. She winked at the younger man who flashed her a broad
smile in return. Roy was amused at his brother.

"I'll have two hamburgers all the way with a side of french fries. Bring me a "Dr. Pepper®, too, if you will," Roy replied quickly to interrupt the blatant flirtation.

"Are your hot dogs good?" The younger man asked while staring straight into the woman's heavily-mascaraed eyes.

"They're the best around," she assured him.

"Well if you say they are, then I'll believe you. Better bring me three, all the way. I'll take some fries and a Coke."

"Onions?"

"Yeah. I don't have a hot date tonight," he laughed and winked.

"Okay, honey. It'll be right out." She boldly returned his wink, turned on the heels of her white leather waitress' shoes, and headed towards the short-order cook waiting at the grill behind the counter. He looked pleased to have something to do to past the time.

"Better watch out," Roy warned. "You'll end up with wife number seven."

"You're crazy," the younger man laughed. "To that? She's old enough to be my mother. I'm just humoring her. You know, making her feel good. No harm in that. And no, I'm not looking for number seven. I've had enough marriage and divorce. Women are bad news."

"Yeah, but you're not fooling me. Besides, you weren't looking for numbers 1, 2, 3, 4, 5, and 6 either. Anyway, you're too young to call it quits. Besides that, you're full of crap." They both laughed knowing Roy was right as usual.

The waitress returned soon with their bottled drinks and placed them on the scarred wooden table.

"Food will be right out. Did you want mustard or mayonnaise?" she asked.

"Mustard on the hot dogs. Mayonnaise on the hamburgers, right?" the young man asked. Roy nodded his agreement.

When she left, Roy took out a pack of Winstons® and a silver lighter from his front shirt pocket. With swift, well-rehearsed movements, he flicked open the lighter and lit the cigarette. Suddenly, the air smelled of lighter fluid and tobacco. He puckered his lips, inhaled deeply, and blew a perfect smoke ring into the air. The brothers watched the white, wispy ring's shape elongate before finally disappearing into the ceiling's darkness.

"Tommy, what happened with Peggy anyway? I thought that would be the marriage that would make it."

Tommy shrugged. "I don't know. She wanted kids. I have three kids by three different women and don't care to have anymore. Always nagging and accusing me of other women. You know how women are. They're never satisfied no matter what you give them or how hard you try to please them. I worked my butt off driving that eighteen wheeler long distance. Gone four and five days at a time, but what did I get? Nagging, fussing, complaining when I got home. Roy, I just ain't gonna live the rest of my life like that. I don't need it. I don't need anybody that much. Especially a woman."

Roy turned and stared at his brother for the first time since he'd started talking. Tommy had struck a nerve.

"Why do you think we feel that way?" Roy curiously asked.

"What way?"

"You know? What you just said. Like we don't need anybody – especially a woman." Brown eyes gazed intently into blue ones. "Do you really believe that?"

"I don't know. I haven't really thought about it. I don't analyze things like you do. Why? What do you think?"

Simultaneously, Roy shrugged his shoulders and shook his head. "I've got my ideas." He deftly held the cigarette between the middle finger and thumb of his right hand and blew smoke into the air above his brother's head. He continued breathing in the intoxicating nicotine until the cigarette was finished. Afterwards, Roy snubbed out the remaining stub and filter among the other gray ashes in a green metal ashtray.

As if it were carefully choreographed, the waitress returned with hamburgers and hot dogs wrapped in white tissue and two small cardboard containers piled high with golden french fries. She plopped a bottle of red tomato catsup on the table between them.

"What else can I get you?" she asked while cocking her right hip forward and hugging the metal tray against her sagging breasts.

"Nothing for now. Everything looks really good," Tommy answered with a flirtatious grin. His eyes never left hers.

She blushed and smiled uncomfortably in response. "Well, you boys just let me know if you need anything else. Enjoy." They both watched as she walked over to the counter and began wiping it with a damp dishrag.

Roy warned his brother, "Don't make me sick. I'm trying to eat."

Tommy just laughed. They drowned the fries with tomato catsup and lots of salt and ate in silence. When all remnants of the sandwiches and fries were gone and they had swallowed the last drops of the cool soft drinks, they relaxed in the booth.

"Pop, do you ever think about it anymore?" the young man timidly asked. He sure didn't want to open a can of unhappy worms and pry into his introverted brother's hidden feelings.

Roy looked down at his hands, now trembling slightly. "What do you mean? Oh yeah. Sure I do." He paused for what seemed an eternity and lit another cigarette. "Of course, I think about it. I've laid awake lots of nights thinking about it and trying to figure out why it had to happen to us. My two girls don't understand why I was raised in an orphanage. You know, it's hard to explain it to them when I don't fully understand it myself."

"Didn't she love us back then?" Tommy asked.

"She says she did. She says that is why she did it."

"I still don't see how she could do that to us. I've spent my whole life trying to feel like I belong to something, like I matter. Even now, I don't feel like I was ever wanted. I feel like the black sheep of the family and always have."

"I can understand how you feel, Tommy. But remember, you're not alone. We all felt that way." He paused before continuing in a low, unsteady voice. "There was only one of us who looked at it as being a positive thing. And that was Richard."

"I thought Mary and Lee were okay with it, too. Weren't they? I know that Lizzie and I were too young to remember home or to really know anything different."

"Well, Mary eventually adapted to it and made the best of it. But she did have a hard time accepting it. Lee? Well you know Lee. He was in heaven as long as he was around girls – any girls, but he hated the work and the discipline. As you know, the place was full of girls, but there was a lot of work and a lot of discipline. Poor Lee found that out first hand."

They both chuckled at the thought of their brother Lee.

"Me? Well, I thought I'd learn to like the place in the beginning. All in all, it wasn't that bad. But it just wasn't growing up on Mercy Avenue like I believe Dad intended for us to do. I was old enough to remember how living in a home like normal kids was all about. And take Mark. He got to go away to the Navy to avoid it. He got to travel and see the world. I guess in a way I held that against him for a long time."

"Yeah, Roy, but think about it. Mark was only sixteen when he was fighting in World War II," Tommy reminded him. "He had to be scared out of his wits, don't you think?"

"Yeah. I know you're right. That did take guts." He gingerly fingered his cigarette and blew another perfect ring of smoke into the air. "You know, sometimes I felt like all I was doing was fighting lots of battles. Fighting a war that couldn't be won. You know, as I recall, I got beat up over you and Lee and Richard every time I turned around."

"It was because you never backed down from a fight, Roy," Tommy cracked. They both chuckled. "Give me one of those cigarettes, will you?"

"Well, I wasn't going to let anyone treat any of you bad. She'd already done that. I guess I felt like I had that responsibility shoved on me. But I really didn't mind."

They grew silent, drifting off to their own separate thoughts and the secret places of their hearts. Roy was becoming uneasy. It was hard for him to keep his emotions in check, so he began fidgeting.

Tommy recognized this and hesitantly asked, "Will you tell me more about him, Roy?"

"What do you want to know that you haven't already been told?" Roy asked.

"I don't know. It's hard to remember much about him after 40 years," Tommy said. "Besides, I'd just turned seven when he died." His blue eyes moistened. Embarrassed, he turned away.

Instantly, Roy understood and felt compassion. He flicked open the lighter, lit another cigarette, and inhaled deeply. After taking a couple of draws and ordering two more soft drinks, he slowly turned to face his younger brother.

"Okay, Tommy. I'll tell you what I remember about him. But it may take a while."

The Single Event

Chapter 1

What lies behind us and what lies before us are tiny matters,
compared to what lies within us.
Ralph Waldo Emerson

Roy: I've relived that awful summer's day in September 1940 so many times I could scream. I wish the painful memory of that day would finally die and go away, forever removing itself from my life - just like he did. No matter how many years go by, the sights and sounds and smells are still real—constantly threatening any long—term happiness I may try to muster, constantly insisting on raising its ugly memory from the crumpled folds of a messy childhood. There is no leaving it behind. No matter how hard you try, you just can't forget the single event that changes your whole life forever—the one that starts the avalanche of subsequent events. It blows away any normalcy you know like the fragile blossoms of a dandelion held hostage by a merciless wind. That is, I sure can't forget it, and God knows how hard I've tried.

The signs of death were all around, submerging us in an unwelcome embrace to the point of suffocation. The simple wreath of white chrysanthemums, garnished with a few sprigs of green foliage, baby's breath, and a white ribbon, hung patiently beside the screened, wooden door of our modest six-room house. A simple wreath in honor of a simple man. It didn't seem fair, though. There should have been red roses for the man who sang "My Wild Irish Rose" to his wife every afternoon when he got home from work. The sterile-looking arrangement acted as a lighthouse beacon in the dark, but this time to beckon unwanted neighbors, uninvited friends, unfamiliar relatives, and lost strangers to our home where it seemed they had no better place to go.

Oddly enough, it was the two conspicuous strangers, the men dressed in dark suits and white shirts with somber faces and carefully combed hair, who moved around our living room at ease. Obviously, they were accustomed to this inevitable event that happens to other people every day. This is how these men made their livings—moving around like zombies, whispering softly into waiting ears, directing actions quietly in the midst of chaotic emotions. I remember detesting them for being in my house on this the first day of school. Why didn't they go somewhere else and take their neatly combed hair and feminine hands with them?

"So, this is how they put bread and butter on their supper tables and feed their wives and little kids," I thought. "I'd rather starve first than be around death all the time. With Daddy gone now, who'll put the bread and butter on our table?"

I scanned the cramped living room with its polished oak floors and the multi-floral wallpaper. My mother's homemade green curtains were puckered together with a vertical row of straight pins to keep out the stifling heat of the afternoon sun. Wall-to-wall people sat on the plump cushions and stiff armrests of the green and yellow sofa and matching chairs. A fat man with a single wisp of gray hair plastered to his sweaty forehead blew stale cigarette smoke rings nonchalantly into the perfumed air. He seemed too relaxed, too comfortable sitting in Daddy's brown leather chair. The low hum of male voices echoed from the white-framed doorways and four corners of the crowded room. Several women dabbed at their eyes and daintily sniffed into monogrammed linen handkerchiefs. But no matter how hard I tried, my eyes were like magnets – never straying far from the walnut casket perched in the middle of the room where my pale-faced father lay motionless.

After a while, I walked past the diverted eyes and headed towards the kitchen where all the women seemed to congregate. Like the ladies' perfume counter in the department store downtown, a mixture of overpowering aromas poured out – ones that I still remember and detest to this day. Our kitchen table was completely covered by a ham with pineapple rings, two roasted turkeys, fried chicken legs, and slices of roast beef. Vegetables and other side dishes were spread all over the melamine countertop—German potato salad, corn on the cob, beans of all kinds, fried squash, sliced tomatoes, cucumbers, home-made breads, and sweet and sour pickles. Stacked on top of the refrigerator were fruit preserves, jugs of tea, coffee, ice water, and lemonade. My eyes stopped when I saw the lemon pie with a mound of browned egg whites — ironically, Daddy's favorite dessert. I felt my eyes burning, so I turned to see a chocolate cake leaning sidewise on an ivory porcelain platter. Juices oozed from an apple pie's brown crust onto a paper blotter. My brown eyes met the sad eyes of Aunt Eliza who had been watching me from a corner of the noisy kitchen.

"Roy, let me get you something to eat, sweetie," she offered.

"Don't want nothin," I stated matter-of-factly. Then, I shrugged my shoulders in a grown-up gesture that was meant to tell her she should worry about someone else for now and leave me alone. I was angry with her, but I didn't understand why. I was angry at the world, and I did understand why.

Normally, my three brothers and I would have been fighting over a drumstick. Only, I wasn't hungry. I didn't even like the smells that were permeating every room of our home. I didn't want to accept their food or the reason it was here. I was beginning to feel sick to my stomach probably since I hadn't eaten anything since breakfast. Not since my Aunt Eliza came to the school to get us before lunchtime on this the first day of the new school year.

I turned my back on her and returned to the living room. For two cents and a stick of gum, I easily could have thrown up in the fat man's lap. That would get him out of Daddy's chair, the one we weren't allowed to sit in when Daddy was home. I smirked and allowed my thoughts to drift back to the morning when the world was still okay and not upside down. I wanted to relive brief, happier events.

Chapter 2

Every life has its dark and cheerful hours. Happiness comes from choosing which to remember.
Anonymous

Roy: "Boys and girls, I think you'll find the fourth grade exciting. We'll learn about so many interesting topics this year, and we'll take a few field trips together."

Miss Allie Greene was the prettiest teacher in New Hanover Elementary School. I was in a trance-like state of mind, hanging onto her every word. Boy was I lucky! I'd prayed every night since school was out this summer to land in Miss Greene's fourth grade class. I'd even gone to Sunday School a few times during the summer just so God would know I was trying to be good, and so he'd answer my prayers. I felt pretty good, because this had to be proof my prayers had been heard and had gotten farther than just the ceiling.

Miss Greene was absolute perfection—tall, lean, young, and pretty. She stood erect and didn't slouch like me. Her hair was blonde and cut in a "bob." The brown seams on the backs of her stockings ran straight up the middle of really shapely calves—not crooked seams like old Mrs. Drayton's, my third grade teacher. But it was her eyes that I fell in love with the first time I saw her. Miss Greene had the biggest, bluest, watery eyes that reminded you of a swimming pool. I felt like I could drown in them, and I didn't care if I did.

When she smiled, her red lips parted to show white, perfect teeth. They weren't bucked in the front like mine. Her smile sent a warm feeling throughout my body that ran from the roots of my dark-brown hair to the tips of my ten-year old toes. I made myself a promise then and there to bring her apples every day even if I had to climb Mr. Kelsey's apple tree to steal them. God wouldn't approve of that, but then again, he might just help me out by sending some wind to blow the apples off the limbs. The plain and simple fact was this—I was head-over-heels in love for the first time in my life. And I was positively sure it would be the first and only time, too.

A hard rap on the door interrupted Miss Greene's lyrical litany. I watched as she floated across the room to answer the obtrusive knock. Our school's principal, Mr. Gardner, was the culprit who dared to interrupt her. I watched as he whispered in her left ear. Turning slowly, almost reluctantly from him, her eyes searched the four rows of wooden desks and chairs until they stopped on my face. I swallowed hard. Her heart-shaped lips were twitching as she forced a smile. I noticed her eyes were teary as I watched them change into dark wading pools. She cleared her angelic throat before calling my name.

"Roy, could we see you outside in the hallway, please?"

"Yes'm." I stood up. I couldn't remember getting into any trouble that morning, but I wasn't exactly in my right frame of mind either. Tentatively, I headed towards the open door where Mr. Gardner stood patiently waiting.

"What a weirdo!" I heard Casey Parks whisper loudly. "Gets in trouble on the first day of school. Whadditellya? I told ya he was a weirdo!" He was laughing and nudging Philip Jones, the red-headed, freckled-faced boy sitting in the desk beside him.

I intentionally crossed in front of their two desks to leave my signature "threatening look" – bring it on buddy, bring it on. When they snickered in reply, I made a mental note that Casey Parks was number two, and Philip Jones was number three on my "beat-your-butt" list. Russell Thomas, our neighborhood bully, still held first place on my list.

"I'll getcha, Parks," I sneered under my breath.

"Yeah? C'mon," he smirked.

"You, too, Jones," I threatened. Jones stopped snickering and looked sideways at Parks. There was hope for Jones; he might be smarter than he looked.

Immediately, I noticed Miss Greene was even prettier

up close than from a distance. She extended her right arm in my direction and placed her hand softly in the middle of my back. Her touch sent a jolt of electricity surging throughout my body. She probably had wrinkled my new starched blue shirt, but I didn't care. I'd made it this far without wrinkling it too bad.

Time seemed to suspend as I came to a new realization. I wanted to be with her for the rest of my life. I'd find a way to repeat the fourth grade as many times as possible. Of course, Mama and Daddy wouldn't like it. They'd be embarrassed to tell their friends that their 18 year-old son was still in the fourth grade, but they'd get over it. I'd find a way to convince them. By then, I'd be old enough to marry her. Sure, I'd have to be patient, but I was well on my way to formulating a sure plan. During the school year, I'd make her like me so much that she was sure to wait for me to grow up. And I'd be a good husband, too. I'd even let her keep on teaching school after we were married. That is, if that's what she wanted to do.

"Roy, please go with Mr. Gardner. Your Aunt Eliza is waiting in his office," she explained.

"What for?" I asked innocently as my thoughts soared. I couldn't believe it! Of all days for Aunt Eliza to mess up things! Today was the first day of school, and I was in love. Besides, Parks and Jones were owed a real clobbering on the playground for embarrassing me. And I was looking forward to morning recess.

She hesitatingly glanced towards Mr. Gardner who just stared. "Roy, you'll need to get your things and go with Mr. Gardner. Your aunt will explain what this is about when she sees you."

"Hello, Roy," Mr. Gardner said, smiling down at me. Wow was he tall! I'd never realized how tall he was.

"Hi, Mr. Gardner," I sheepishly replied and swallowed hard. Unfortunately, we had many shared memories, so this couldn't be too good. I turned to Miss Greene.

"I can't remember doing anything on the bus to get into trouble. Do I have to go home?"

Parks laughed audibly.

"You're not in any trouble, Roy," she said with a smile.

"Well, I didn't, didn't bring nuthin', nuthin' to school t-to-day, bein' it's the first day an'—well ya know—bein' the first day an' all," I stammered. My tongue felt fifteen times its normal size, and my mouth felt like it was stuffed full of cotton balls. I couldn't even speak plain English when she was around. How was I going to marry her?

"That's fine. You run along, Roy. We'll be thinking about you." She patted my shoulder this time. I didn't know why there were more tears pooling in the corners of her big blue eyes. But I knew I'd be thinking about her, too.

"I'll be back tomorrow," I assured her. I didn't want to make her cry.

She hesitated, "We'll see you soon, Roy."

As she turned to close the classroom door, I heard Casey laughing again.

"Yeah, a paddling wouldn't hurt him any," he laughed loudly. I turned quickly towards him, but Mr. Gardner's strong hands firmly caught both of my shoulders and steered me down the hallway.

"Let's go to my office, son."

I made another mental note to replace Russell with Casey on my "beat-your-butt" list.

Mr. Gardner didn't talk to me as we slowly walked down the vacant hall towards his cluttered office. For whatever reason, I noticed Aunt Eliza was wearing a green dress and black open-toed heels as I entered the office. It was obvious she had been crying, because her eyes were red and puffy. She managed to flash me a quick smile but quickly diverted her eyes towards my brothers and sister who sat on Mr. Gardner's brown-leathered sofa. Mark and Mary looked scared. Lee and Richard looked dumb-founded like I felt.

"Children, your Aunt Eliza is going to take you home. Your mother needs you to come home now, so your aunt is going to take you. We'll see you in a few days." Mr. Gardner was rambling. He seemed nervous and unsure of what to say next. "And we'll be thinking of you all."

He looked awkwardly over at Aunt Eliza and smiled. Neither one met our perplexed stares. I glanced sideways at my oldest brother, Mark, and wondered why he wasn't saying anything. His eyes were focused on his new dress shoes, but he was sniffling loudly. Aunt Eliza motioned us outside and led us to her parked car without saying a word. This was strange to say the least.

All the way home, she sat stiffly and stared straight ahead at the two-lane paved road. There was no idle chatter, no laughter like normal. My mama's youngest sister was the prettiest aunt in the bunch, unmarried and my favorite. I was crowded in the backseat between my two younger brothers, Lee and Richard. Mary and Mark sat in the front seat of the shiny, black 1939 Ford. When we turned into our driveway, I suddenly realized what this was all about. Subversive thoughts, the kind you shove as deep as possible because they are fearful and unwelcome, began surfacing. My heart knew the truth even though my mind tried to lie. The truth would become the reality I would have to face. I'd known this moment was coming for a long time.

"Reverend Small wants to talk with ya'll. I'll see you in the house," Aunt Eliza stated before walking quickly up the steps and into our home.

There was no escaping reality and no escaping Reverend Small.

Chapter 3

Forgiving means to pardon the unpardonable and loving means to love the unlovable. Or it is no virtue at all.
G.K. Chesterton

Roy: I had noticed when Aunt Eliza parked the car in front of our house on Mercy Avenue, the dirt street was lined with unfamiliar cars and trucks of all makes, models, and colors. Aunt Eliza had opened her heavy car door and scurried across the freshly cut grass up the five short steps to the porch, leaving us standing reluctantly behind—not wanting to go in to face the truth we already knew and didn't want to hear. Our mama's minister, Reverend Small, opened the screened door with a grim face. He motioned for us to join him on the wooden porch. I had never liked him even though he was a preacher.

    Reverend Small always smelled funny, like a lady. I'd bet my week's allowance that he even wore ladies' perfume or ladies' cologne. His hands were soft and pudgy, too, not rugged or callused like my Daddy's strong hands. When I pointed out all his faults after church one Sunday, Mama explained that well-dressed, professional men smelled like that and usually had soft hands because they didn't do manual work. Well, from that point on, I didn't plan to be a professional man if I was going to turn out like Reverend Small.

    He sat down in the middle of the porch swing and patted the vacant spots on either side of the seat. Richard and Mary joined him while Lee and I stood on either side of Mark. As he wiped his sweaty forehead with a wrinkled handkerchief, he kept his beady eyes focused on Mark.

    "What's goin' on, Reverend?" Mark asked impatiently. "Tell us why Aunt Eliza got us out of school and why you're here. It's Dad, isn't it? Is that why all these cars and trucks are here? Where's Mama? Are you going to tell us or continue to make us wait?" Mark's face was red, and he was close to tears. "Where's Mama?"

"Son, I'm going to tell you. Your mama is all right. Nothing has happened to her. She wanted me to explain this to ya'll. So I will." He paused and cleared his raspy throat. "Unfortunately, I do have some bad news for you children."

"Then it is Dad, isn't it? Has something happened to Dad?" Mark asked. His voice was rising. He was losing it.

Reverend Small had hesitated too long. He tugged uncomfortably at his bright green tie. "Son, why don't we go inside where it's a little cooler. Aren't you hot? I'm hot. It's really stuffy out here. Let's go inside, and I'll tell ya'll."

I'll never forget the way he looked on that particular day-perspiring, uncomfortable, and fidgety. He led us towards the back bedroom where Mary and our youngest sister, Lizzie, shared a room. The wall-to-wall multitude of curious and sympathetic onlookers quickly and quietly moved aside to form a pathway. I remember how slowly and grimly the five of us moved through them like we were headed for a spanking. I was reminded of a Sunday School story where Moses parted the Red Sea – only I felt like the sea was drowning us. It's strange how I still can remember some of the surrealistic details of that moment.

Three year-old Lizzie, named after Aunt Eliza, sat in Aunt Penny's lap sucking her right thumb. Dark baby curls circled her olive-skinned face. She was sleepy and whiny – probably because she'd missed her morning nap. Aunt Penny, Mama's eldest sister, looked like an owl because the big, black-framed glasses she wore covered up her round face. Tommy, our youngest brother at five months, was nursing a bottle of milk Reverend Small's wife, Martha, was feeding him. For a split second, I envied being younger like Lizzie and Tommy. There was something else I remember about Reverend Small that day. His voice was high-pitched, monotone, and matter-of-fact when he told us the bad news like he'd done this a thousand times before. I remember it this way. After we walked into Mary and Lizzie's room, he closed the door.

"Children, have a seat on the bed."

"We're not allowed to sit on the bed after it's made up," warned Mary. "Mama will get mad."

"It's okay. She'll understand this time," Reverend Small reassured us. He cleared his throat and turned his broad back to us as we sat timidly, waiting on the edge of the blue bedspread. He clasped his pudgy hands behind him and lifted his round head up towards the ceiling the same way he did every Sunday when he paused to make a special point. "Children, your father died this morning around 11:00." Then he softened his voice, turned to peer at each of us, and said, "His suffering is finally over. Your father is gone to Heaven to sing with the angels. He's laughing and singing with Jesus and the angels right this very minute. He's happy. He's not sick anymore. You believe this don't you?"

Our heads bobbed up and down mechanically. So, it was true. Our sub-conscious fears were true. Daddy was gone forever. Slowly, it sank in.

Reverend Small continued after pausing briefly to acknowledge our mute reactions to his inquisition. "Good. I know this hurts deeply, but it is really the best thing for your daddy. He wasn't ever going to get well. He was suffering, and now his suffering is over. Aren't you glad that it's over for him? I am, praise the Lord. Yes, I'm sure that one day you will learn to be glad, too." He paused before beginning again.

"That's a stupid question for me to ask. I know you're glad his pain and suffering is over. And I know you're going to be strong and help your mother get through this. She needs strong little soldiers to help her get through this terrible loss. Remember the hymn we sing on Sundays, 'Onward Christian Soldiers'? You'll have to be strong Christian soldiers for her, because your mother is taking this very hard."

Suddenly, his attention was focused on my grief-stricken brother, Mark, whose shoulders were shaking with sobs. But Reverend Small didn't let up any, no not an inch.

"Son, look at me. Look at me, Mark. You've got to be

the man of the house now. You'll have to help your mother and these children now that your daddy's gone. You have to set an example for them. Your daddy would expect that from you."

Mark raised his head and met Reverend Small's intent stare. He looked like he wanted to spit. I pitied my brother and hated this messenger of bad news. Who did Reverend Small think he was? Why did Reverend Small say this was the best thing to happen? Why couldn't Daddy have gotten any better? To me, that would have been the best thing. Not dying would have been the best thing. Why did Daddy have to get sick in the first place? Why didn't Russell Thomas' daddy get sick or someone else's daddy? Why did our daddy have to die? Maybe Reverend Small thought this was the best thing to happen, but he didn't live in this house. He wasn't going to miss Daddy like we were. And what about our feelings? How were we supposed to act? My ambivalent feelings tore me in half. Should I be selfish and cry like I wanted to do, or should I try to be strong like I was being told to do? After all, I was only ten years old, and this was new to me. It was new to all of us!

I remember the suffocating lump in my throat and the sudden wave of sadness that washed over me. As tears began pouring from the corners of my eyes, a loud scream stifled my mounting sobs. My throat ached and my empty stomach churned as I held back my own sadness. We all did. Mama's pain erupted in the form of wails and screams.

"Randall! Oh my God! You can't leave me alone! I need you, Randall. Please don't leave me." She pleaded and cried the same words over and over again.

How could anyone cry so much? Where were all her tears coming from? When could we cry? I heard grief in its purest form and felt it in the bottom of my soul. When I couldn't stand it any longer, I tore through the rooms and stormed out of the house, slamming the screened door behind me.

I ran from the zombies bringing food and false smiles.

I ran from people who were watching us closely and making mental notes of our reactions.

I ran from Reverend Small's monotone voice and his bad news.

I ran from his fat wife.

I ran from my brothers and sisters and their grief-stricken stares.

I ran from the screams and cries of my mother.

I ran from the death that engulfed us.

I ran and ran and ran until I doubled over from sharp pains in my right side and until my lungs threatened to burst.

It was the stop sign at the end of our dusty dirt street that supported me.

Chapter 4

*If all our misfortunes were laid in one common heap whence every-
one must take an equal portion, most people would be contented to
take their own and depart.*
Socrates

Roy: I wrapped my little arms around the sign's four-cor-
nered post and held tight. Here, beneath its morbid, authoritative stare, I opened my soul to drain the contents of my
ten year-old boy's heart. When I couldn't cry any more tears,
when I couldn't scream any louder, when I couldn't hurt any
longer, I stopped and allowed a calming peace to replace my
sadness momentarily. I used the sleeve of my shirt to wipe my
swollen eyes and dripping nose. Slowly, my knees buckled,
and resigned, I dropped to the ground.

For years, this stop sign had represented one of the
boundaries in our little world. Mama and Daddy always had
cautioned us to play in the neighborhood but not to go beyond the stop sign at the end of the street. For us, our im-
mediate world consisted of eleven framed-houses, six on one
side of the street, five on the other side and an overgrown
weedy field where we played ball.

The stop sign with its octagon red face was where I
ran to meet my father's work truck every afternoon. He was
always punctual—5:30 on the dot. I'd met him here for as
long as I could remember. That is, until two months ago when
Daddy had moved to the American Red Cross Sanitarium. He
had a disease called tuberculosis or "TB" for short.

Aunt Eliza had tried to prepare us for the worst.
Around the end of July, she warned us that Daddy may never
come home again and that God had plans for him in heav-
en. When we told Mama, she got mad at her for telling us
"such lies." None of us could understand, much less accept,
how final this disease might be. I hoarded up all the hope I
could and believed that miracles, magic wands, fairy tales,

or prayers would provide a happy ending. I prayed that God would change his plans for Daddy in Heaven. I promised to be good for the rest of my life. I even promised to quit eating candy or chewing gum. I promised to go to church every Sunday for the rest of my life. I promised anything and everything. It seemed so odd that God would answer my prayers to be in Miss Greene's room and not to keep Daddy from dying. This had to be a mistake!

Salty tears started again as the truth crept back to the forefront of my thoughts. Daddy would never meet me here again. I'd never hear him whistling "My Wild Irish Rose" or feel his callused hand ruffling my hair. He'd never spank me again. I'd even settle for that. Living in an adult world was overwhelming and sad.

Yes, Reverend Small, I cried loud, and I cried for a long time on that September Monday. The only witness to my grief was a stop sign that stood tall, erect, and at attention. It honored the passing of a ritual shared by a beloved father and his young son. The stop sign that ordinarily flaunted its authority didn't tell me to be strong. It remained silent, still, and patient. Somehow, I knew it understood the loss I was suffering under its watchful guard far better than you did.

Chapter 5

The way to happiness: keep your heart free from hate, your mind from worry, live simply, expect little, give much.
Barney O'Lavin

Roy: When I reluctantly returned home, my mama's three brothers, Uncle Ralph, Uncle Bob, and Uncle Thomas, were standing on the front porch with their left hands shoved deep into the pockets of their best Sunday suits. They kept their right hands free for shaking those with the strange people lining the sidewalk and heading towards our front door. I heard them using the same phrases over and over again.

"Hello. Thank you for coming."

"How are you? Yes, this is sad. We're all very sad."

"You're right. Randall was a good man. He will be missed."

I hurried past their collective stares and broke through the line of adults waiting to enter my house. But I wasn't quick enough, because a worried Uncle Ralph grabbed my arm and pulled me aside.

"Roy, come here son," he whispered. "Your daddy's lying in the front room. They brought the casket a few minutes ago. Just wanted you to know before you went in."

"Are you okay, son?" asked Uncle Bob who peered over Uncle Ralph's right shoulder.

"Yeah. I'm all right," I answered with a quick shrug. Uncle Thomas opened his arms and started towards me, but I dodged him and hurried to the door. I wasn't in the mood to be hugged and didn't know when or if I ever would be. I diverted my eyes from the casket.

Aunts were swarming around the kitchen like bees on a honeycomb. They fixed plates of food for guests and tried unsuccessfully to persuade my silent siblings and me to eat. I noticed the guests' china plates were piled high enough to feed two or three of us for a week. We'd never gone hungry in our lives, but with nine mouths to feed, the word left-over was not a common word in our vocabularies.

I returned to the living room, but I didn't look at the casket—not yet. Mark was talking to Aunt Penny and had a strained look on his pale face. He awkwardly shifted his weight from one foot to the other. He was struggling to be strong and to hold back the tears. I pitied my big brother who had Daddy's strong chin and Mama's black hair. Just that morning, he had been excited to begin his first day at New Hanover High School. His first day of high school would be a sad memory for the rest of his life.

Mary, who was two years older than me, silently sat on the floor at Aunt Jeannie's feet, Daddy's eldest sibling. Occasionally, Mary listened to what Mark was saying. I watched her wipe a stray tear with a crumpled handkerchief. Aunt Jeannie leaned forward and stroked Mary's long, dark hair. Often, I pitied Mary because Mama depended on her to help with the housework and to care for the two younger children. While the rest of us got to play hide-n-seek, marbles, horse races, and other games after school and during the summer months, Mary had to help Mama. Of all the children, Mary favored Daddy the most. She had his dark-brown, curly hair, his Irish blue eyes, and his straight white teeth. She was a looker, and all the boys in the neighborhood were starting to notice—especially Johnny Perkins, the boy next door. I knew he'd be here now if he wasn't still at school.

Lee, my younger brother, was eight and had a carefree attitude. He was easily manipulated because of his naïveté. He was the most handsome boy of our small clan.

"Lee, you're gonna be a lady's man," Mama would say with a laugh. "You're just like your Papa." Lee had a way of saying just the right thing to coax Mama out of giving him a whipping. It never seemed to work for the rest of us, but it did for Lee. He had Mama's black eyes and olive complexion, Daddy's brown, wavy hair, and Uncle Ralph's humor. Lee always had a joke to tell. But today, he looked baffled, bewildered, and terribly out of place. Lee's agitation reminded me of a wild caged animal looking for the quickest way out. He stood in the corner of our living room trying to be invisible. I started to join him when I noticed Richard talking easily and freely to Reverend Small.

There was something special about six-year-old Richard. He easily conversed with adults on various topics, quickly made friends with kids his own age, and enjoyed caring for younger children. Often he stayed in the house and helped Mama and Mary with Lizzie and Tommy. He was the most intelligent, the most precocious, and the most religious person in our family. Our mama was religious, but Richard had her beat. And adults in the family whispered that he had the gift of prophecy because he was born with a veil over his face. I'd never seen it, but they said it was true.

When Sunday mornings found the rest of us lazily lying in bed milking the last moments of precious sleep, Richard arose early, dressed quietly, and helped Mama fix our breakfast. Mama "made" us go to church. But she didn't have to make Richard. He enjoyed going to church so much, he probably could invent a reason for going every day.

If you asked the brown-haired, brown-eyed boy what he wanted to be when he grew up, Richard would proudly respond without a minute's hesitation, "A preacher. I'm gonna be a preacher when I grow up. Reverend Richard is what they'll call me."

Fine with me. I just hoped he'd be a better preacher than Reverend Small. Richard had learned more of the Catechisms than the rest of us put together. As a daily ritual, he read the small captions and studied the pictures in Mama's Bible. One day, when Richard was four, Mark was looking for his history textbook. He found Richard lying on the living room floor leafing through its pages. That's when he began teaching Richard how to read. He read better than me. Richard was smart and learned everything quickly.

On special occasions like Easter or Christmas, Daddy

had gone to church with us. I'd pinch, hit, or kick anyone just for the privilege of sitting beside him. And as you can guess, I usually managed to get my way. Mama, the exception, was always on Daddy's other side where he could hold her hand or place his arm around her shoulders. I loved to hear my father's deep baritone voice as he bellowed out the various hymns Reverend Small had selected for Martha, the church's musician who alternated between playing the organ and the piano, to play. Once in a while, Daddy would look down as he sang, catch me watching him, and wink.

"I know all about the Good Book that I'll ever need to know, thanks to my mama. She made us go to church every Sunday while my ol' man slept," he'd respond whenever Mama begged him to go to church with us. "Mama can't read a lick, but she sure can quote the Bible word for word—even better than Reverend Small. And believe me, I've heard scriptures all my life," he'd laugh. "She'd quote us Bible scriptures right before we got a whipping. And that was quite often, I might add," he'd chuckle.

My train of thought was broken by Richard's voice. "Reverend Small?" Richard beckoned.

"Yes, Richard," Reverend Small replied with a smile.

"Reverend Small, 'Whispering Hope' is one of Daddy's favorite hymns. He taught me the words. Do you want to hear it? Do you think Daddy would want me to sing it for him now? Do you think he could hear me if I sang it?"

"Sure, son, uh, that is, if you feel like singing," replied the Reverend, looking somewhat baffled by Richard's innocence.

Richard smiled at his reply. He shoved his tiny hands into his pockets. He cleared his child-like voice, lifted his eyes towards the ceiling, and quieted the room with the sincerity, awe, and inspiration of a child.

"Soft as the voice of an angel,
Breathing a lesson unheard,
Hope with a gentle persuasion
Whispers her comforting word;
Wait till the darkness is over,
Wait till the tempest is done,
Hope for the sunshine tomorrow,
After the shower is gone.
Whispering hope,
O how welcome thy voice
Making my heart in its sorrow rejoice."

If there were any dry eyes in the room, they found a wet release at last, while the teary-eyed found a new reason to cry. Amidst broken hearts and the welling up of a flood of tears, a small boy smiled towards Heaven and "whispered hope" for those left behind to mourn our father's passing.

Yes, that was Richard, and Richard was our special gift.

Chapter 6

*No one has ever seen God; but if we love one another, God lives in us
and his love is made complete in us.*
I John 4:12

Richard: When Daddy died, I was six years old and starting
school for the first time in my life. I was excited about the
first day of school and being in Mrs. Ray's class. She had been
Roy's favorite teacher until Miss Greene. I'd learned a long
time ago that if Roy liked someone a lot, then they must be a
pretty special person. So unfortunately, my first day of school
began happily and ended sadly.

Some men brought Daddy's coffin to our home late
that afternoon. Lots of folks had come to pay respects to our
father. Well-known and well-liked in the community, he'd be
embarrassed over this big fuss everyone was making. They
had dressed him in a dark suit and tie, and anyone who knew
Daddy knew he didn't like wearing a suit and tie. Only Daddy
didn't move a muscle. He just laid there with ghostly white
hands crossed over his still, lifeless chest. I remember wishing that he'd sit up and tell one of his jokes so that the aunts,
uncles, cousins, grandmothers, neighbors, and church people
could laugh.

"I didn't know there were so many Deacons at the
church," Roy said while scanning the room. "And look at all
those men over there from the lodge. What is a Moose Lodge
anyway?" Eventually, Roy would come to like the Lodge men
who served as honorary pallbearers. For days and months after the funeral, they brought us food, candy, and occasionally,
gum.

It was too hot and too sad to sleep that night, so Roy
and I went outside to sit on the porch swing. I don't remember
talking about anything; we just watched the stars and cried
together, which was special to me. Even though Roy was a
person of few words, I usually could figure out what he was

thinking. He was so patient and mature with me that night. Once or twice he put his arm around my shoulders and let me lean against him to cry. He just stared towards the end of the street or looked up at the twinkling stars. In his own special way, I knew he was talking to Daddy. I was, too, in between talking to Jesus. You know what I'm talking about. It's when you think words in your head and mean them in your heart. You don't have to speak them aloud. I wanted Jesus to know that even though I was really sad, I was glad Daddy wasn't hurting any more.

Around lunchtime on Tuesday, the funeral men came to take Daddy to the church. We all started crying again, especially Mama. Uncle Ralph and Uncle Thomas supported her on either side as she leaned over and kissed Daddy goodbye. Her legs kept buckling under her like dishrags in a kitchen sink, so they gently placed her in Daddy's leather chair.

"Look at that poor young widow," one of the neighbor ladies said.

"Roy, why did she call Mama a window?" I asked.

"She didn't call her a window. She called her a widow."

"What does that mean?"

"I think it means she's not married anymore."

Aunt Jeannie gathered us together and pushed us towards the casket to say goodbye. She told us to go in the order of our birth—oldest to youngest. Some people don't like to touch dead people, but I didn't care. I knew this would be the last time I'd touch him. Patiently, I waited for my turn.

Mark stared at Daddy for the longest time and wiped his dark, swollen eyes with both hands. He reached down and covered Daddy's hands with his own before going to stand beside Uncle Russ.

As Mary approached our lifeless father, I noticed her hair was uncommonly tussled and not combed. She began crying so loudly, Aunt Eliza came over to gently lead her away.

It was Roy's turn. I really wondered what Roy would do since he hadn't cried all morning. I'd heard our aunts and uncles whispering about him acting "a little odd." I knew Roy wasn't acting any odder than he normally did. They just didn't know that Roy was a private person who kept his thoughts and feelings to himself unless he was mad. Then he didn't care who knew it. That was Roy.

Roy's small steps reminded me of a game we sometimes played, Mother, May I? I knew Roy would rather be fighting with Russell Thomas, the neighborhood bully, than doing this. I saw him turn to Uncle Ron for encouragement.

"Go ahead, son, and tell your daddy good-bye. This is your special time."

Even though Uncle Ron looked mad, he wasn't. Uncle Ron had deep wrinkles in his forehead, so whenever his busy eyebrows touched together, he looked mad. He nodded his head again, "Go ahead, son. Take your time."

Roy grabbed the casket's polished wood with both hands. He stood there for the longest time without moving, without crying. Our aunts and uncles looked at each other. They didn't know what to think. Finally, Roy turned away and sat on the couch. No tears. It was the same "Roy" face you'd expect to see when he was happy or sad. Roy just wouldn't let anyone get inside him. He just sat there, staring at the floor our father had laid, sanded, and varnished.

Lee went next. He looked pitiful as he shuffled towards the casket. Once there, he began crying loudly.

"Daddy, please wake up. Tell me another joke. Please don't leave us. Okay?"

He cried the same words over and over until Aunt Jeannie pulled him towards her. When Lee's face landed smack in the middle of her big bosom, I gasped aloud. Everyone looked at me. I just knew Lee was going to suffocate and die! Aunt Jeannie's chest almost smothered me once. She never realized how dangerous she was or when to let you go.

I remember Mama telling Daddy, "If Jeannie's brain

was as big as her chest, she'd be one of the smartest women alive."

"You're just jealous," Daddy would say with a chuckle. Then he'd playfully grab at Mama, and they'd start laughing.

To my relief, Aunt Jeannie finally let Lee go. I heard him gasp for air before she led him to the sofa. She plopped down beside Roy and tucked Lee in her arms where she rocked him back and forth like a wee baby, just like Tommy. When my eyes glided over to Roy, I noticed he was smiling. How could he be smiling on Daddy's burial day! Then it dawned on me why he was smiling. Poor Lee. It was kind of funny after all.

"Richard, go ahead," Aunt Jeannie whispered. "It's your turn to say goodbye."

I was ready. I drug an ottoman over to the wooden box where I could peer inside. Daddy looked so calm, so peaceful, so quiet. He wasn't coughing anymore or spitting up blood. We'd watched "TB" do that to him. The way his mouth was pinched together made him look like he was smiling. When I kissed his cheek, I immediately noticed how cold he was. That was a real shock because I remembered how warm it used to be when I kissed him. Reverend Small said Daddy had become an angel in Heaven with wings and a halo. He said Daddy always would watch over us like a guardian angel does. To me, Daddy had always been an angel – just one without wings.

"Daddy, I love you," I whispered in his right ear. "I always will – and I know you'll always watch over us like you promised." I knew he heard me.

I brushed away a tiny tear as it trickled down my face and checked to see if I'd upset Mama. She was muffling her cries in a handkerchief. I didn't want to make her any sadder than she already was. Everybody had reminded us to be strong for Mama, and I didn't want to let her down because of my sadness. I remembered their words.

"You have to be strong for your Mama."

"You need to be a smart boy, and be good for your

Mama."

"You children have to be brave."

"Your mother will need your help."

"You have to be good children."

In my heart, I knew we'd be okay. Daddy was an angel, so he could fly around and watch over us. I patted his head just like he used to pat mine. Then I turned my back to the man I'd always love and remember.

Uncle Russ carried Lizzie over to Daddy, but she started kicking and screaming. He took her outside on the porch and calmed her down by rocking her in the porch swing. Tommy, unaware that we'd lost our father, was asleep in Aunt Penny's arms. We had said our good-byes like we were told to do. Then the funeral parlor men asked Aunt Eliza to take us to another room. She quickly herded us into Mary and Lizzie's bedroom to wait for the casket's closure and removal.

When I turned to leave the room, Granny's violet blue eyes caught mine. She had the same blue eyes Daddy had. Her penetrating stare filled me with love and comfort and gave me the strength to not cry. She smiled sweetly and approvingly before dabbing her eyes and nose with a man's handkerchief. There was nothing dainty and prissy for Granny, Daddy's beloved mother. I faked a small smile because I felt really sorry for her. Granny had lost her son. Even though Uncle Russ and Uncle Ron and Aunt Jeannie were still around to love her and help her, Granny's life would never be the same. She had outlived a child – something no parent ever wants to do. I watched this strong oversized woman waddle over to the casket to touch her son's lifeless face for the last time. Then I went into the bedroom to wait.

Pre-Event Life

Chapter 7

God allows us to experience the low points of life in order to teach us lessons we could not learn in any other way.
C.S. Lewis

Roy: The spring and summer months before Daddy entered the sanitarium started off innocent and carefree. Tiny azalea buds became fragrant blossoms that colored our world with the likes of an artist's pallet of pastels. As the days grew longer, our patience grew shorter for school to be out. We were ready for three careless months without books, full of tireless play, trips to the nearby beach, and childhood mischief that we were experts in creating. We began our week long spring vacation eating corn flakes and bananas for breakfast. As soon as we were finished, Mama shooed us out of the house, so she and Mary could begin the daily ritual of household chores. Mama couldn't wait to wash our clothes in the new wringer-washer Daddy had brought home from Sears and Roebuck the Saturday before.

"Randall! This is a wonderful surprise!" Mama exclaimed.

"Nothing's too good for my best girl. Come here and give me a kiss." Daddy beamed as Mama planted a big kiss square on his lips.

Colicky Tommy was always crying, needing a bottle, or pooping in his cloth diapers, so we were glad to escape the confining house. Everyday, Mama would quote her favorite Proverb as she locked the door to prevent us from running in and out of the house and making a mess.

"Cleanliness is next to godliness. So, that's why I keep a clean house," she'd remind us daily.

And she did. Neighbors used to say, "You can eat off Iris' floors. Her house is so clean. Never a speck of dust anywhere."

So when we wanted a drink of water, we had to knock.

If Mama was in a good mood, she'd fetch it for us, or if she was in a bad mood, she'd yell, "Go outside to the spicket and get it."

Going to the bathroom was easily solved, too. Being boys, it wasn't a hard thing to take care of. Lee and I taught Richard to just whip it out whenever you had the urge to go.

"Just aim it anywhere you want to. In this direction or in that direction," laughed Lee. "You can even water the flowers like I do." Richard watched in awe as Lee demonstrated his well-practiced skill.

For Lizzie it was a little different since she didn't have anything to whip out. So, we taught her to go behind a bush and squat. A couple of times, we forgot to tell her to pull down her underwear, so she'd walk around with wet pants until they dried. Boy did she smell bad! We all suffered when that happened, and we all agreed it must be hard to be a girl!

"Girls have to be prim and proper," Lee stated. He posed with his hands on his hips and a scowl on his face. "I'm glad I'm a boy. Don't have to worry about finding a bush when ya really gotta go. Just whip it out and aim. Got that, Richard?"

"Yeah, Lee. I think so."

Being a quick learner and with me as his "main" teacher, I didn't anticipate Richard having any problems. Lizzie on the other hand, well, maybe it wasn't all her fault. It would take time.

One day after playing under the house with our metal cars and trucks, Lee and I crawled out to find Richard and Lizzie on the front porch playing dolls. When Richard would dress one of the dolls, Lizzie would remove its clothes, and Richard would have to start all over again. This went on for a while until I became nauseated.

"We've got to do something about that," I whispered to Lee.

"What do ya mean?" Lee asked.

"Playing dolls. Boys aren't supposed to play dolls.

Look at him. He acts like he likes it, too. We're falling down on the job. If we'd played dolls with Mary, Mark would have walloped both of us. Know what I mean?"

"Yeah, you're right, Roy. We've gotta do somethin' about it. Whatta ya want to do?"

"I don't know." Then an idea hit me. "Let's play horse races!" I yelled.

"I want to play! I want to play!" Lizzie screamed with utter delight. "I want to be a jackie! I want to be a jackie! Go horsey go." She never could pronounce the word right.

"It's jockey, Lizzie. You want to be a jockey," Richard reminded her.

Lee and I always were the horses, and Richard and Lizzie always were the jockeys. The rules of the game were simple. We'd start at the front porch steps, and only I could yell, "Go!" Whichever horse and jockey made it around the house, circled the magnolia tree in the front yard once, and made it back to the front steps first won the race. We loved the game and played it for hours if the horses held up.

"Okay, I've got Richard, so you've got Lizzie," I ordered. Even though Richard weighed more than Lizzie, I always chose him as my jockey. I was afraid Lizzie's underpants might be wet, so I never chose her. Lee hadn't figured that out yet, so he went along with the familiar selections.

"I'm a stallion," I yelled.

"I'm a pomaranian," Lee yelled back.

"That's a dog, you idiot!" I laughed. We all laughed as Lee's face turned crimson.

"Well, I got mixed up," Lee said with a sneer. "I'm whatever horse starts with a 'p'."

"I can think of several words that begin with a 'p' that you are, "I replied. "Besides, you mean Palamino."

"Then I'm a Palamino," Lee agreed with a shrug. "That's what I meant the first time."

Lizzie and Richard stood on the top step, so they could easily mount the horses.

"Bend down lower, Roy, so I can git on," Richard pleaded. It was hard for him to climb onto my back.

"All right, all right. Just keep your pants on." I was in a bad mood with the doll stuff and all, so they should hope that we'd win, or my mood was going to get worse.

I watched as Lee picked up Lizzie up with one arm and easily swung her onto his back. Even though Lee was two years younger, he already was three inches taller than me.

"Whee!" Lizzie laughed. "Go horsey, go horsey, go! I'm a jackie! Look, Richy, I'm a jackie!" By now, she was kicking poor Lee in the ribs with both of her dirty bare feet.

"Okay. Ready, set, go!" I yelled and took off with my jockey bouncing up and down on my back.

"I wish I had a real saddle and spurs," Richard yelled.

"Are you crazy? I'm glad you don't," I wheezed over my shoulder.

"You're right. Better forget about the spurs."

Four races later, we'd only won once. I was panting and sweating hard and mad because I didn't like to lose. Everyone said I was the most competitive one in the family.

"It ain't fair!" I yelled angrily to Lee. "Richard weighs more than Lizzie. No wonder ya'll win all the time. I could win if I had five pounds of potatoes on my back instead of a jockey almost as big as I am!"

"You're the one who picked Richard. I didn't. You always pick Richard, anyway. You're just mad because you lost fair and square," sneered Lee who didn't seem intimidated by me anymore. I'd have to fix that. He kept on with that smug-looking smile on his face. "You're jest not as fast as I am. Gittin kinda slow in your ol age, huh Roy?"

"Oh yeah? I'm gonna wipe that smug, stupid smile off'n your ugly face." In a flash, my nose was two inches from Lee's. "I'll show you how to respect your elders."

"Roy, that was what Reverend Small's sermon was about last week! You were really listening!" Richard cried. "He's right, Lee. We're suppose to respect our elders."

Richard's innocent excitement startled me. I forgot what I was doing and just stood there dumbfounded watching his happy face. But Lee knew how to quickly bring me back to my senses.

"Yeah? You and who else? Lizzie?" challenged Lee.

"What do you mean? I can beat your butt in two winks!" I challenged.

"Sure. It won't be you by yourself!" shouted Lee.

Boy, did Lee have the nerve! I'd given him more than one bloody nose to go along with a couple of black eyes.

"Hey, Roy, Lee. C'mon. Don't fight," Richard pleaded. "I know. Let's play marbles instead."

"Mind your own business," Lee said and spat in the dirt.

"Don't talk to him that way," I said with a sneer.

"Oh yeah. He's my brother, and I'll talk to him any way I want to."

"No you won't."

"Well, we'll jest see about that."

We stared defiantly into each other's eyes. Neither one of us had any intention of backing down. When I shoved Lee's shoulder as the first physical challenge, he just started laughing. He held up both of his hands in a surrendering gesture.

"Next time, ol man. Next time." Lee headed towards the outdoor spicket to get a drink of water.

"Scaredy cat. Daddy raised a scaredy cat," I mocked him.

"C'mon, Roy," Richard pleaded again. "Leave him alone. C'mon. Let's play marbles."

As Lee bent over and drank water from the silver spicket, I drew lines in the dirt with my big toe, the one I'd stumped the other day on the porch step. Mama said my half-black toenail would probably fall off. Lee and I couldn't wait until it did, so we could see what was under it. No one we knew had ever lost a toenail. Reluctantly, I shrugged my shoulders and gave in.

"Okay, let's play marbles. I'm too tired to fight, anyway. Besides, it's too hot," I agreed.

"Good idea," Richard replied. "Marbles seem like a better idea to me, too."

"Besides, this was all about you, anyway," I explained.

Richard had a puzzled look on his face. "About me? What did I do?"

"Nothin'. You didn't do nothin' 'cept play dolls with Lizzie. You're a boy, Richard. You can't play dolls with Lizzie all the time."

He hung his head. I thought he was going to cry, and that was something I didn't want.

"I just want what's best for you, that's all. Know what I mean? You're a boy."

"Roy, Lizzie has no one to play with. If I don't play with her, who will?"

Good question and one I certainly hadn't considered.

"She needs someone to play with. You have Lee. Mama has Mary. I have Lizzie. Besides, she needs someone to take care of her. When I play with her, that makes her happy. Sure, I like boys' games better. Besides, dressing dolls ain't all that bad."

Sometimes, Richard could make me feel two inches tall. This was one of those times. To save my face, I answered, "Well, I was just worried about you. That's all."

Richard beamed and hugged me around the waist. "You don't have to worry about me ever."

With temporary truces made between Lee and me and Richard and me, we climbed under the house to play marbles. This time, we included Lizzie. The framed houses' foundations on our street were raised and supported by brick pillars without underpinning. With plenty of room to crawl and sit up, "under the house" was our favorite place to play and beat the spring heat and enjoy shade. The cool dirt could become roads and hills in a matter of minutes. And being under the house offered an advantage point over the neighborhood bullies. From our vantage point, we could see out on all four sides of the yard. That way, Russell Thomas and his gang of troublemakers couldn't sneak into our yard without us knowing about it.

Richard drew a circle and poured out his marbles. Lee added his. I watched as Richard carefully studied his shots. Man! His aim was pretty accurate most of the time. I could see this game was going quickly downhill for Lee. Just yesterday, Richard had won Lee's favorite Cats Eye when they were playing "for keeps."

With a brick pillar for support, I lazily leaned back and stretched out my legs. Besides, it was going to be fun watching Lee get his butt kicked in a non-violent way. Yeah, this was gonna be a fun spring vacation.

Chapter 8

Blessed is he whose transgressions are forgiven, whose sins are covered. Blessed is the man whose sin the Lord does not count against him and in whose spirit is no deceit.
Psalm 32:1-2

Richard: Sometimes the urge for mischief spontaneously occurs without any preliminary deliberation. It begins as a tiny voice inside your head that gets more intense every minute. The more you try to ignore it, the louder it yells that it's here to rescue you from being "too good" for "too long." You can't concentrate on anything else, because this temptation becomes a chigger begging to be scratched. You want relief from this itch, but you're not suppose to scratch. So you hum a song, you play a game, you recall a favorite Bible verse, like "do unto others as you would have them do unto you." But this itch penetrates all the good you know, and resistance is gradually worn away. You give in and you scratch. This is true even for sweet little boys who don't always enjoy being known as a "goody-two-shoes" that no one wants to play with.

On a spring day when all my siblings were at school, the urge for mischief grabbed me from behind without warning. The constant nagging of a younger sister can do that to you! I was known as the sweet and innocent child. The "good" child who was smart and who never did anything bad.

But today, I deserved some quiet time to look at Bible pictures. I needed relief from an itchy little millstone for just a few minutes. That's all. The millstone was my younger sister, Lizzie. When I succumbed to the itch and scratched, when I caved in, when I gave it up, you know, when I couldn't handle it any more, I changed the course of a rather mundane day in 1940.

We'd begun that day no differently than the long, endless multitude of days before it – the ones lost in the innocence of being a young child with no responsibilities. Nature's artistic touch painted the bright mornings of my childhood. Robins and sparrows chirped loudly in the budding trees as they spied bumble-bees and honey-bees. These noisy creatures searched hungrily for rich nectar offered by multicolored flowers that lined the front of our house. Occasionally, a car's engine broke the humdrum of the lazy morning as it slowly drove down the dusty, dirt street in front of our white framed house. Mama was busy washing breakfast dishes in the kitchen sink. The pink-walled bedroom that my two sisters shared was decorated with freshly-starched, white lacy curtains Mama recently had made. This room was located in the back of our house. Solemn-faced stuffed animals sat motionless in the middle of the four-poster double-bed that had once belonged to Grandma, our maternal grandmother. Two naked baby-dolls laid forlorn and abandoned on a corner of the blue cotton bedspread. It was in this familiar and inviting room that I scratched my itch. This room would soon become my three-year old sister's temporary prison.

Lizzie had all the looks from birth. Her eyes could melt the heart of a tyrannical king. Everyone who visited our home instantly fell in love with the tiny human who would quickly grace their laps, suck a wrinkled thumb, and say dumb things to make them laugh. Little did anyone care that she peed in bed every night, occasionally sucked a bottle, and couldn't pronounce my name right.

"Richy! Richy!" she hollered from morning till night. Why with four other siblings did she choose my name?

"Richard. My name is Richard, not Richy." I'd tried to teach her.

And like all other little brothers and sisters, she could be a demanding, nagging little monster. It seems that only big sisters and big brothers discover this fact. Adults seem oblivious to it. By then, it's too late for parents to return younger siblings to the hospital. Too bad little brothers and sisters didn't come with money-back guarantees. Anyway, I really didn't want to get rid of Lizzie. I just wanted a few minutes of quiet time to do what I wanted to do.

On this morning, I'd endured all I could take of her constant, whiny, demanding, little voice. My patience was worn thin. I couldn't take a step without her following along behind me. For the past three years, my family had endured her pointless crying, her smelly diapers, spitting up, learning to crawl and peeing in her training pants. I used to wonder why Mama and Daddy felt the need to get Lizzie and now, Tommy. I had been the baby for three glorious years. I was potty-trained, cute with dimples, and knew how to drink out of a regular cup without spilling anything. Why in the world would two relatively smart adults want to go through all of that again? And why did they want all the rest of us to go through it with them?

So with these thoughts and my frustration, I succumbed to mischief. I decided once and for all to scratch this itch good. I'd simply lock her in the bedroom for a few hours while I read my book. Little did I know what commotion this would cause.

Cleverly, I lured her into the bedroom. It didn't take a scientist to know what to do. I dangled her favorite doll in front of her greedy eyes. Her plump little hands reached forward to grasp the doll.

"Give it to me, Richy. Give it to me," she begged. Her eyes never left the doll.

While I temptingly suspended the doll in mid-air, I backed slowly towards the door. At the last minute, I threw the doll onto the bed. It landed on the farthest side from the door. As she shuffled to retrieve it, I turned the lock and slammed the door! No more little sister for a while! I was free! I'd envisioned her crawling onto the bed, sticking her thumb in her mouth, and quietly napping for a few hours. Was I wrong!

I have never heard such excruciating screams and shrill cries come out of the mouth of a person so little! My short-lived smile of satisfaction was replaced by the sudden awful realization of what I'd done. My thoughts were momentarily frozen. What had I done? We'd need a key to open the door, and the key was in the lock on the other side of the door with Lizzie.

Abruptly, my mother stopped washing dishes and rushed into the room.

"Richard! What's wrong? What's wrong with Lizzie?" she cried.

I slithered into a nearby corner beside an end table and lamp and tried to blend into the room. I put on an innocent face. "Think fast," I thought.

"She must have shut the door and locked it," I stuttered. I felt bad, because this wasn't the truth.

"Richy, wet me out. Wet me out!" she wailed.

My mother who was faster than a speeding bullet and able to leap furniture and scattered toys with a single bound was across the room in a flash, turning the doorknob back and forth. She pounded helplessly on the door. Then I realized there was no way of getting Lizzie out! What were we going to do?

Well, initially, Mama panicked. I panicked. Lizzie was already panicking. Soon, my screams and cries matched those of my baby sister. What had I done? What made me lock up a three year-old in a room without any way of getting her out? No matter how aggravating Lizzie could be, she didn't deserve this.

"Don't cry, Richard. We'll think of something. Stand here and talk to her. See if you can calm her. I'm going outside to look through the window," Mama said before running out the door.

"Lizzie, Lizzie, don't cry. Don't cry." I heard my voice repeating itself. "Don't cry, Lizzie. We'll open the door." When I wondered?

"Lizzie? Do you want to play a game? Come over here and talk to Mama at the window." Mama's voice even made me feel better.

Lizzie stopped crying. I could hear her footsteps moving away from the door and towards the window.

"Mommie!" She started crying again.

"Don't cry, Lizzie," Mama soothed her. "Let's play a game."

The crying stopped.

"When I tell you to come to the door, can you come to the door? Good! When I tell you to come to the window, can you come to the window? Good girl! Okay, Mama's going back inside the house, okay?"

No reply.

Mama hurried into the kitchen and began rummaging through different drawers. A drawer and its contents crashed loudly to the floor. I felt like the heel I was. I deserved to have a spanking. I even wanted a spanking, because maybe it would make me feel better.

"Keep talking to Lizzie, Richard. Keep her calm," Mama yelled from the other room. Mama was dialing a number on the telephone. Lizzie could have all my favorite toys.

"Hello, Ralph? <Pause> I need your help. I can't get in touch with Randall. Lizzie's locked herself in her bedroom. <Pause> Yeah. I don't know how. Can you come over and help me get her out? <Pause> Okay. See you in a bit. Bye!"

Mama returned outside and coaxed Lizzie to the window. Lizzie started giggling.

"Mommie! Peek-a-boo! Peek-a-boo!" Lizzie squealed.

After a while, the giggles on the other side of the door grew quiet. Fears began racing through my mind. Why was she so quiet? Was she okay? After all, Lizzie wasn't that bad when you thought about it. She was okay to play with sometimes. Whenever we got candy or desserts, she never finished, so I got to finish hers. I ran outside where Mama stood on tiptoes looking through the window.

"Is Lizzie okay? Why is she so quiet?" I cried.

"She's fine," Mama reassured me. She beckoned me over to her. "Come here and let me lift you up. Shhhh. Be quiet."

Mama lifted me so I could peer inside the window. I cupped my hands around my eyes to block out the sun's glare. Lizzie's little body lay framed between the lacy curtains. She was curled up on the bed with her thumb in her mouth, fast asleep.

By the time Uncle Ralph arrived, I was feeling better. Quickly and seemingly without effort, he removed the door's brass pins and hinges. I held my breath as he lifted the big oak door to free my sister from her temporary prison. Rushes of happiness, relief, and guilt ran through me. Lizzie was okay, she was free, and she was my little sister whom I loved. On that eventful morning, I silently vowed to always protect her.

That afternoon, I admitted my guilt to Mama. I'd already admitted it to Jesus. After a menial scolding – not Mama's usual – I was sent to my room to stay until Daddy came home.

"Your father can decide if you're punished anymore. I know you feel bad, Richard. It's just not like you to pull a stunt like this. I hope you've learned a lesson. Because Lizzie is so young, she could have gotten into something and gotten hurt. Now go to your room and don't come out until Daddy gets home."

When Mark, Mary, Roy, and Lee got home that afternoon, I heard Mama whispering. Then there was silence. I heard more whispers before my brothers' familiar footsteps headed towards the cramped bedroom we shared. Mark entered first with Lee nudging him and peering anxiously over his shoulder. Roy lingered behind in the doorway. Mark and Lee's solemn faces were quickly changed by two big smiles. Mark stacked his schoolbooks on top of the oak dresser, winked, and hurried out. Lee threw a spelling book onto the double-bed he shared with Roy. He shook his head back and forth, chuckled under his breath, and waited for Roy to enter the room.

As usual, I couldn't read Roy's expressionless face as he held my gaze. Finally, he sauntered over to where I miserably sat on the bed. He shifted his textbooks from under his right arm to under his left and placed his right hand firmly on my shoulder. He squeezed it and lowered his face so that it was level with mine. His eyes were penetrating as he said in a low, steady voice, "I'm proud of you, boy. That took a lot of guts."

Chapter 9

The events in our lives happen in a sequence in time, but in their significance to ourselves, they find their own order...the continuous thread of revelation.
Eudora Welty

Roy: With the school days ticking away slowly like the hands on a wind-up clock, Mrs. Drayton had selected me to take the attendance record to the school's office and to pick up our ice cream treats for morning break. Getting to go to the office and bring back the ice cream was a big deal back in those days.

"Hello, Roy." Mrs. McFarland, the school secretary, greeted me slowly. "Are you here to see Mr. Gardner again?"

"No, ma'am. Mrs. Drayton sent me to give you the attendance record and to git our ice cream order." Her shoulders relaxed. She seemed relieved.

"Good!" she answered cheerfully, and extended her hand to take the report. "Let's go across the hall to the supply room. That's where we keep the freezer and the ice cream."

Before we headed out, Mr. Gardner appeared in his doorway with his eyeglasses perched low on his nose. "Hi Roy. Here to see me?" He bent to retrieve some papers from Mrs. McFarland's desk.

Gee! What was the deal? Why did everyone assume I'd done something wrong to warrant a visit to the principal's office?

"No, sir. I'm here to give Mrs. McFarland the attendance report and to pick up our ice cream order," I replied matter-of-factly. They had me mixed up with Casey Parks. He practically lived in the principal's office.

"Good boy. Keep up the good work. Mrs. McFarland, I need to dictate a letter when you get back."

"Okay. I won't be long," she replied with a smile. She was a really pretty lady whose husband had died a long time ago. Sometimes, I wondered if she got lonely.

I followed Mrs. McFarland's tall, slender figure to the storeroom across from the office. Its walls were covered with white shelving on which books, paper, boxes of pencils, erasers, and other supplies were stacked.

"Is Lee glad that first grade is almost over?" Mrs. McFarland asked.

"I think he'll be relieved to have summer vacation." I hoped I sounded grown up and conversational.

"I'm sure," she giggled. "Lee seems to be a smart little pupil. He's got the cutest smile."

"Yes, ma'am." Lee smart? I'd have to re-check his report card at the end of the school year.

"Does he like having Mrs. Beard as his teacher?"

"I'm not sure. I guess so." I knew that Lee didn't like Mrs. Beard. Besides, Lee didn't like school. That was one thing we had in common.

"Here. Let me see Mrs. Drayton's order."

She took the paper and began placing the cold pop sickles and fudge sickles in a cardboard box. I thanked her and headed down the creaky hall lined by institutional green, bare walls. I'd pass Lee's classroom ahead on the right, so I planned to look inside at Lee and stick out my tongue. Perfect! The door was wide open. I slowed my pace and began tiptoeing so Mrs. Beard wouldn't notice me. I sneakily peered inside the doorframe and saw Mrs. Beard scolding a frightened first-grader. His eyes were as big as saucers as he stared into the stern teacher's face. I quickly searched until I found Lee's desk. Empty! Quickly, I scanned the room. He wasn't in the room. Where was Lee?

Disappointed, I began to tiptoe away. After I'd taken a couple of quiet steps, I heard someone whisper my name. It was Lee!

"Roy. Roy. I'm over here."

I looked over my shoulder. No Lee. Where was his voice coming from? Where was Lee? I stopped to listen again.

"Roy. Here I am."

I peered at the small crack between the door and the doorframe. Lee was standing behind the door with his nose in the corner. One eye is all I could see.

I got closer and pressed my mouth to the crack. "What are you doing behind the door?" I demanded.

"Shhh! She'll hear you!" Lee cautioned me in a loud whisper.

"What are you doing behind the door?" I demanded the second time.

"Mrs. Beard put me here for talking," he reluctantly replied.

"What?" At first, I thought it was funny. Then I became dumbfounded. How dare that old battle-ax put my little brother in the corner and behind a door at that!

"Please don't tell Daddy and Mama," Lee pleaded. "Please, Roy. Don't tell on me."

I knew Mama would probably let it slide like she normally did when Lee got in trouble. But not Daddy. No way! He believed in behaving and discipline.

"If you can't do anything else, you better behave in school. And I expect you to do just that," he'd warned us.

I knew all too well what Daddy's spankings were like. So did Lee.

"Just be quiet, and don't git into more trouble. We'll talk later on the bus."

The box of ice cream was getting colder by the second. I'd better hurry back to the classroom, or Mrs. Drayton would make sure I saw Mr. Gardner for other reasons. As I climbed the stairs of the old brick school building that led to my second-floor classroom, I contemplated what to do. I couldn't believe anyone, especially mean ol' Mrs. Beard, would do that to my little brother. Who did she think she was? Lee was talkative, but he didn't deserve the embarrassment of standing behind a door where everyone could see him.

I panicked! Everyone could see Lee standing behind the door. Everyone knew Lee was my little brother. So obviously, everyone would conclude that he was following in my footsteps. Mama and Daddy would blame me for setting a bad example. It would be my fault – not Lee's – that he was turning into a juvenile delinquent.

I'd reached the stairway landing when I finally calmed down. Another idea dawned! Maybe no one had to know, certainly not Mama and Daddy. Besides, it was difficult for me to actually see Lee behind the door. This could be a blessing in disguise. Granny was always reminding us to count our many blessings. Well, this was one that just landed in my lap without any effort on my part. I would use it for my own good. Since Lee was scared to death Daddy would find out about this embarrassing situation, I'd become his ally. Besides, I really didn't like it when Lee got spanked any more than I liked it when I got spanked. But Lee didn't have to know I felt that way, and he wouldn't.

A smile crossed my face as my plan was born. On the bus ride home, I'd check to see if Mrs. Beard had sent a dutiful explanation note home to our parents. If so, the note would somehow get "misplaced." Surely Lee would agree, and this would become a shared secret that would go to our graves with us.

Now as to chores. What summer chores? My blackmail would ensure that I'd have a summer free of chores, thanks to Lee. What a wonderful blessing and one that I'd count on for a long time!

Chapter 10

We live by faith, not by sight.
2 Corinthians 5:7

Richard: The first day of summer vacation was a special time in our young lives. On this particular day, Mark had caught a ride into town with Daddy that morning. He was going to be a paperboy and sell newspapers on the corner of Market and Front Streets downtown where Daddy's shop was located. I'd never seen Mark so excited about anything. I was happy for him. He deserved the opportunity to make some spending money for himself. Mama didn't waste any time asking Mary to help her with the household chores and Tommy. At least Mary would be inside out of the heat, and Mama was certain to keep the attic fan running and a few oscillating fans going to circulate the warm air.

I started the day playing dolls with Lizzie. She declared me the "daddy" and she was the "mommie." Whenever I dressed one of her dolls, I never did it exactly right, so she'd scold me and remove the clothes for me to start all over again. Later that morning, Roy, Lee, Lizzie and I played "races," one of our favorite games. I was getting too heavy for Roy, but for some reason, he insisted I was his jockey. He always did, and I didn't mind. But when we didn't win any races, Roy and Lee almost got into another fight. Luckily, they stopped before someone ended up with a black eye. Usually, Roy won all the fights, but Lee had grown a lot this past year. Frankly, I wasn't sure who would win now.

Later we went under the house to play marbles and to beat the squelching heat. Hearing Mama and Mary's voices and footsteps above our heads made me feel guilty about playing and not helping them instead. Marbles was my second favorite game. Over the year, I'd gotten pretty good with my aim and shots. By now, I'd won about five of Lee's favorite marbles.

"Hey Roy," Lee said. "Did'ya hear Mama and Daddy last night?"

"No," Roy replied. I think he was almost asleep. "What were they talking about?"

"I dunno. They really weren't talking. It's what they were doing. I've heard them lots of times. Doggone it! I should have made that shot!" Lee shouted.

"Keep your mind on your game, or Richard's gonna own all your marbles." Roy closed his eyes again.

"I will. But do you know what were they doing?" Lee insisted.

"Well, since I didn't hear what you're talking about, I don't know what they were doing."

"It sounded like they were squeaking the bed on purpose. They were giggling a lot and doing a lot of whispering."

Roy asked, "Why were ya bein' nosey, Nosey?"

"I'm not nosey. Besides, it was hot last night, and I couldn't sleep."

"Yeah. I do know what'ya mean. I heard them last week. I asked Mark about it, and he gave me the scoop."

"What scoop? Tell me."

"Why should I?" Roy asked.

"Because you should."

"What's in it for me?" Roy teased.

"I dunno. Nothin'. Besides, I'm already doing all your chores," Lee replied. He sat still for a minute, then he picked up his favorite blue marble – the one that I hadn't won from him yet.

"Here. I'll give you this marble if you tell me."

"I dunno. I don't really like the blue one. Give me the red one over there, and I'll think about it."

"Oh no. You've got to promise to tell if I give it to you."

"All right, cry baby. It's a deal. I promise."

Reluctantly, Lee grabbed the red marble and tossed it towards Roy. Roy picked up the marble and slowly raised up on one elbow to answer Lee. With a serious look on his face, he turned his head from side to side to ensure no one else was listening. Then he began talking really low.

"All right, then. According to Mark, it's a game adults play. They sit on the edge of the bed and take turns seeing who can make the bed squeak the loudest."

"You're kiddin'?" Lee asked.

"Cross my heart and hope to live." Roy crossed his heart and held up his right hand. "I swear. That's what Mark told me, and Mark never lies."

"Seems like a crazy game to me," Lee said and shook his head.

"Yeah, to me, too. But here's the real scoop," Roy paused dramatically for effect. By now, Lee had inched closer to Roy. I stopped aiming and gave him my full attention, too. Even Lizzie was listening intently. "Mark said that after they play this game several times, they usually get a baby."

"A baby? Not another one! We don't need another baby in the house!" Lee gasped dramatically.

"I know. We've already got Tommy, and that's all we need," Roy agreed with a nod of his head and a shrug of his shoulders.

"Where would we put another baby?" I asked.

"Nowhere," Lee quickly answered. "Besides, how does playing that silly game get them a baby?"

Roy whispered again, "Well, after they play that game for a while—say a couple of months or so—they usually get tired of it and go to some cabbage patch to pick out a kid they want."

"Cabbage patch! Why a cabbage patch?" Lee was bewildered. "I hate cabbage. Why would anyone go to a cabbage patch to get a kid?"

"I hate cabbage, too," I added.

Roy ignored me and answered Lee. "I don't know you,

moron. I didn't make up the rules of the silly game. Anyway, do you wanna know the rest or not?"

"Sorry. I wanna know," Lee acquiesced.

"Well, Mark says they go to this cabbage patch and pick out the baby. You know, boy or girl. Sometimes people pick out more than one at a time. They're the crazy ones."

"You're kidding? I'd rather go to a pumpkin patch or a cornfield to get one. Pumpkins and corn taste a lot better than ol' cabbage," Lee asserted.

"Yeah, me, too," Roy agreed.

"Is that it?" Lee asked.

"Yeah, that's it," answered Roy a little dejected.

"Wow!" I exclaimed. "So that's where Lizzie and Tommy came from. Wonder where this cabbage patch is?"

"I don't know, Richard. And don't forget, we all must have come from a cabbage patch," Roy added in a matter-of fact tone.

"Roy, do you think that's why Tommy smells so bad all the time?" Lee asked.

"Yeah, probably. I hadn't thought of that. You're right. He must have eaten a lot of cabbage while he was waiting for Mama and Daddy to come and pick him out. Answers a lot of questions for me."

"Do ya think they would have gotten him if they knew he was gonna cry and poop all the time?" Lee questioned.

"Probably. Besides, they'd already made one mistake."

"Whatta ya mean? What mistake?" Lee asked innocently.

"Well, evidently they went to some weird cabbage patch to get you," he said with a laugh.

"Ha ha. That's not funny." Lee looked like his feelings were hurt.

Roy laid back and continued laughing. "Yeah, everyone's entitled to a mistake now and then. It appears Mama and Daddy made two – you and Tommy."

"Gee. Adults sure are weird," I injected. "Do you think we have to grow up and turn into adults?" I asked.

Roy stopped laughing and sighed. "Sure we do, Richard. It happened to Mama and Daddy, so it'll happen to us. That's just life. Count on it."

"You're smart, Roy," I replied with admiration. "How'd you get to be so smart?"

He shrugged. "I don't know. Not everyone can be so lucky."

Chapter 11

As life is action and passion, it is required of man that he should share the passion and action of his time, at peril of being judged not to have lived.
Oliver Wendell Holmes, Jr.

Roy: One lazy Sunday afternoon in early June, the hazy sun kept us from playing outside in the hot, unbearable humid heat. The air was still and everything was too quiet. Many of the neighborhood kids had gone to the beach for the day to cool off. I was angry that we'd had to attend church that morning instead of spending a fun day at the beach. Reverend Small always put me in a bad mood. And along with this heat and no one to play with, I was in a foul mood.

Mama was in the kitchen reading a magazine and listening to bluegrass music on the kitchen radio. Lizzie and Tommy were taking their afternoon naps, so she had some quiet time for herself. Richard was visiting our neighbor, Mrs. Johnson, and probably eating gobs of her famous chocolate-chip cookies. Mary and Mark had gone to Grandma's house for a weekend visit and were due back tonight.

I sat in a side chair and watched a monotonous brass, oscillating fan turning back and forth, mechanically blowing air directly onto our sleeping father. It wasn't doing too much to cool the rest of the room. There was no air conditioning back then except at the movie theaters. People flocked to the movies on Fridays and Saturdays just to beat the summer's heat. Daddy was stretched out on the living room sofa in a sleeveless t-shirt, khaki-colored pants, and white socks. His big toes and heels peeped through two small holes and worn threads in both socks. He snored softly through parted lips.
Completely bored, I walked into the bathroom and opened the medicine cabinet just to see what was inside. Immediately, the red fingernail polish caught my eye. Curious, I picked it up and unscrewed the lid. About that time, Lee came strolling

through the house and walked into the bathroom.

"Whatta ya doin? Gonna paint your fingernails red? Well do it later. I gotta go to the bathroom!" He whispered rather urgently.

"Hold yer horses," I cautioned. "Don't wake up Daddy."

"What are you doing with Mama's fingernail polish?" he asked.

"We're gonna paint Daddy's fingernails!" I laughed.

"Are you crazy? Git outta here so I can pee," he demanded.

"Go ahead. What's ever stopped you before?" I stuck my head outside the door and looked both ways. Nothing. Quietly, I closed the door. "We're going to paint Daddy's fingernails." I had that mischievous twinkle in my eyes. Lee started giggling.

"Hey, it might be fun after all. There's nothing else to do except get our butts whipped." He had finished and was washing his hands. "I don't think this is one of your best ideas. Do it by yourself."

"Shush!" I cautioned him with a frown. "You're gonna wake him up. Besides, you're going to help. It's always me who has to come up with the ideas. So, uh, the least you can do is help me out and go along with my plans. Besides, he might like to know what happened in Mrs. Beard's class."

Lee didn't hesitate. "All right. I'll do it."

With my brother close behind, we tiptoed through the living room and to our sleeping father who was currently emitting an awful, nasal snore. Daddy's whisker-stubbled chin was turned uncomfortably and rested on his heaving chest. More than once, Lee stepped on my bare heels. I winced and shot him warning looks.

Before plunging into our plans, I had second thoughts, but they only lasted a few seconds. Gently, we both moved each of his ten fingers into position. Lee went first and painted his left hand. My brother's talent impressed me. He was masterful at staying within the boundaries of each nail. Next it was my turn. Unfortunately for Daddy, I didn't share the same talent. The fingernails of his right hand, as well as the surrounding skin, were painted bright red by my nervous, hurried strokes. Astonishingly, his snores never wavered.

After we finished, we stood back to admire our handiwork. Not too bad! When we wagered a look at each other, we started giggling. The more we tried to muffle our giggles, the louder they got until we were lying in the floor laughing uncontrollably. Daddy awoke with a puzzled look on his face.

"Wha...What's goin on?" He asked through half-closed eyes.

We laughed even harder. He opened his eyes wider and saw his nails. His face was suddenly as red.

"What have you done?" He demanded. "You two are in big trouble! Iris, come see what your little heathens have done to me!" He coughed once or twice.

Our laughter stopped like the water outside in the spicket when it was turned off.

Mama came running, "What's wrong? Randall, what is it?"

Daddy thrust both hands into the air. "Look!"

"Oh my God! Are you bleeding? What's wrong with your hands?"

"No, I'm not bleeding!" He shouted. Then he pointed to us.

"That's what's wrong with my hands. Your boys have painted my fingernails red."

Mama's worries were quickly replaced by a big smile that grew into out and out laughter. "My boys? Sure. They're my boys when they misbehave. If you ask me, they take after their father." Unfortunately, Daddy wasn't the least amused.

"Well, I don't ever remember painting my papa's fingers red! He'd have used his belt on me if I pulled a stunt like this. I'm thinking about doing the same thing if this stuff isn't off my fingers in a few minutes."

Mama's face froze. "Oh no! Oh no!" She stammered.

"Oh no, what?" Daddy demanded.

"I'm out of polish remover. I ran out the other day. I haven't been to the drug store to get any."

Lee looked at me. By now, we weren't laughing. This no longer was a joke! This was a tragedy, and we were scared to death! We searched the medicine cabinet high and low to ensure Mama hadn't somehow overlooked a drop of polish remover in the house. We had to come up with a solution, and we had to do it quick!

"Let's try this rubbing alcohol!" Lee exclaimed.

"Yeah. That should work!" I agreed.

After thirty minutes of soaking and scrubbing his fingernails with no positive results, we were afraid to look Daddy in the eye. We tried peroxide. We tried bleach. Nothing worked. Daddy's face was almost the same color as his fingers.

Three hours later, Uncle Bob brought Mary and Mark home from Grandma's. They found us sitting on the floor, each with a metal fingernail file that we'd been using to scrape his nails as fast as we could go. Daddy fussed and reminded Mama how she needed to teach her boys some manners. They were laughing when Uncle Bob said with a big smile, "Like father, like sons. Chips off the old block."

I almost caught Daddy grin in response, but that was quickly replaced by a menacing look that sent a clear message to me. If looks could kill, Lee and I would be mincemeat served up in a big flaky piecrust. Daddy was not only seeing the color red, he was seething the color red.

Chapter 12

All things are possible to him that believes.
Mark 9:23

Richard: Granny, Daddy's stout Irish mother, had white hair and a heavy Scot-Irish brogue. She always was a welcome addition to our home, because she brought energy, laughter, and love with her when she came. Granny was known for her hearty laugh and astute knowledge of the Bible. She was adored as much by Mama as she was by Daddy. Even the neighborhood kids excitedly anticipated her quarterly visits. Russell Thomas, too. They had learned that in addition to her other qualities, Granny possessed one more special talent. Granny could tell the scariest ghost stories you'd ever heard. Her tales were guaranteed to make your hair stand on end and to send endless cold chills down your spine.

So when Granny visited us in mid-June, five neighborhood friends, Barry, Jeremy, Johnny Perkins, Todd, and Teresa joined us on our front porch. We huddled closely together, anticipating Granny's slow arrival to the porch swing. The porch swing was only big enough for Granny because her ample body spilled over and took up all the space on both sides. That's why we all sat at her feet. We held our breath as her beloved brogue led our imaginations through dark and frightening places that night. What a sight we must have been with our eyes threatening to pop right out of their sockets, our knees tightly hugged to our chests, and our dirty toes curled under. She introduced us to the strange world beyond - the macabre.

"Let me tell you, little lads and lassies, about the ghost of Cameron Corner. As the tale goes, the ghost didn't have a head. But when he came looking for it each night, you better watch out," she said in a low, slow voice.

There was dead silence, forgive the pun. We were afraid to peer over our shoulders for fear the ghost would be standing behind us. No one said a word. We were too scared to move.

Then out of nowhere, Daddy's booming voice made us jump.

"Who wants ice cream?" Daddy asked. Mama was holding a cooler of homemade ice cream that he and Mama had hand-cranked on the back porch.

Shouts of, "I do, I do," pierced the silence and drowned out the constant crickets' chirps and the sporadic frogs' croaks.

"Good! Cause you've never had any strawberry ice cream until you've had Iris'. She makes the best strawberry ice cream there is!" Daddy boasted.

Mama blushed. "Randall, you're silly."

"No. Just honest. Mary, help us pass out the ice cream. Make sure everybody gets some."

"Yes, sir!" Mary jumped to her feet and eagerly filled our shaking hands with cups or bowls of ice cream and silver spoons.

"This is so good!" Teresa exclaimed. "Strawberry is my favorite flavor."

"I'm glad you like it, Teresa," Mama replied.

"Mama? Are you and Daddy gonna have some?" I asked.

"No, Richard. Ya'll enjoy it. Daddy and I are going for a moonlit walk," Mama smiled.

"And I'll get my sugar that way," Daddy laughed.

"Randall! You're awful." Mama looked embarrassed. "Mother Anna, he's incorrigible!"

"I know. I know. Just like his father," Granny laughed.

Mama and Daddy left us sitting on the dark porch sharing the rich, cold cream with our friends and Granny. What a treat! Ghost stories and ice cream. We knew the neighborhood kids were envious of us, and we basked in that feeling. When Granny was around, everything was special. Even Daddy seemed to be coughing less and laughing more.

But the ghost stories weren't free. In return, we'd have to promise to read her the Bible the next morning. That's all the payment she ever asked for. Lee and Roy thought reading was boring, so Mark, Mary, and I paid that wage for the rest of us. Granny and I sat together for hours the next day while I explained the stories behind each picture in Mama's Bible. She seemed genuinely pleased and patted my head just like Daddy did.

"Thank you, Richard. So until the next time, give Granny a kiss goodbye," she said with a twinkle in her eye.

When Daddy and Mama left to take Granny to the train station that night, I was really tired and sleepy, so instead of waiting for my parents to return home, I said goodnight to everyone and went to bed. After I climbed between the crisp, white sheets, it wasn't long before my eyelids grew heavy.

****

Sometime during the night, I found myself tugging at Mark's limp arm.

"Mark. Mark. Wake up! Please wake up!"

"What is it? Leave me alone, Richard. I need my sleep." Mark buried his head deeper into the soft pillow.

"Mark. Wake up. I saw a woman," I whispered.

"A woman? Where?" he asked curiously. Now his eyes were open, and I had his full attention. He turned over on his right side and faced me.

"I saw a woman in a black dress. She just glided over to the side of my bed and stood there looking down at me." My bottom lip was quivering as I pointed to the spot where she had stood.

"Calm down, sport. It's okay. There isn't a woman in here, especially one wearing a black dress. You must have been dreaming. Go back to sleep."

"I saw her, Mark. I wasn't dreaming. I woke up to go to the bathroom, and she just came over to the bed and stared down at me. She wasn't smiling either." My stomach was knotted up, but I didn't look in the direction the woman had appeared.

"Richard, there isn't a woman anywhere in this room. And if she was, she's gone now. It's probably Granny's ghost stories that you're thinking about."

Even though I nodded, I knew I had seen the woman. "I need to go to the bathroom."

"Do ya want me to go with you?"

I nodded again.

"Okay. Come on."

Mark patiently waited outside in the dark living room for me to finish. He left the bathroom door open, so we didn't turn on the light. After we climbed back into bed, I thanked him.

"Mark, can I curl up closer to you?" Before he could reply, I'd already done it.

He laughed. "Yeah. Forget that it's about 70 or 80 degrees in here. It's okay."

Soon Mark was asleep again. I lay shivering alone in our bed watching and waiting for the lady in black to make her appearance again. I said a little prayer that made me feel better. Finally, I drifted off to sleep. Jesus answered my prayers. The lady in black never visited me again, but I knew she had been real.

Chapter 13

No man can live happily who regards himself alone, who turns everything to his own advantage. You must live for others if you wish to live for yourself.
Seneca

Roy: "Hey, look!" shouted Lee. "Look over there!"

"What are you yellin' for?" I asked.

"Over there!" Lee replied while pointing towards the back left corner of the house. "What's that piece of paper over there beside the bricks? You think Russell is challenging us to a game of ball?"

After breakfast one day, we'd climbed under the house to beat the heat and to play. A sure way to get my attention was to mention Russell Thomas, so I didn't wait. I pounced on the crumpled, yellow piece of paper that seemed really old. With trembling hands from sheer excitement, I opened the corners without causing further damage to the delicate-looking find. Burnt marks appeared on the edges of the yellow paper, and the corners were jagged and torn.

"Look! Oh my gosh! Oh my gosh! Wow!" I couldn't believe I was looking at a map. Lee peered over my shoulder. "You're not gonna believe this, Lee! Hey guys! It's a treasure map! It's a real treasure map!"

They gathered closer around me as I sucked in my breath. It was almost as if I thought breathing would cause the fragile paper to disintegrate. Even Lizzie seemed to realize something important was happening. She held a naked baby doll under her chubby left arm and sucked her dirty right thumb. It was her stand-by thumb when the left thumb was all wet and wrinkled, as it currently was.

"Wait a minute, wait a minute," Lee cautioned. "This doesn't make any sense at all, Roy. As many times as we've been under the house, why haven't we seen a treasure map before now? I think it's a set-up. I betcha Russell's behind it.

Him and his gang are probably watching us now and laughing their heads off."

We all peered out into the four corners of the yard. Nobody was in sight.

"Oh yeah? And what if it's gen-u-ine, Lee, and Russell don't know nothing about it?"

"I don't know," Lee replied.

"Maybe someone lost it, Lee. Who knows? Besides, who cares? We have it now." I gazed intently at the map. "Look! The treasure is buried close by. You're not gonna believe this! It looks like it might be buried somewhere around the big oak tree at the end of the road. You know, the one across from the stop sign."

"What, in all the weeds?" Richard asked.

"Yeah."

"There might. be snakes around there," Richard reminded us.

I didn't like snakes either.

"True, Richard. But that's probably why they put the treasure there. Did you think about that?" My response even impressed me.

"Lemme see," Lee stated. "Who'd bury treasure close to a bunch of houses? That's kind of stupid, don't ya think?"

"I don't know, and I don't care. If they're stupid, that's their loss. But, I'm gonna go find it. Are ya in or are ya out?" I challenged Lee.

"I'm in."

"Okay! So shut up and listen to me. We can't let anyone know about this. Lower your voice and don't act suspicious. Go git Daddy's shovel, Lee. If anyone stops ya, don't tell them nothin'. If anybody tortures you, you better not spill the beans, or I'll spill yours." I was a born leader.

We all stared at each other and nodded in agreement. When Lizzie began to whimper, Richard hugged her so she would stop. This could be dangerous! I was getting a little afraid. Then Richard closed his eyes and began praying aloud.

His timing was perfect.

"Dear Jesus, please keep us safe, and don't let any snakes bother us. We're afraid of snakes and we want to find this treasure. Thank you for letting Roy lead us. He's real good about ordering us around and knowing what to do. Thank you for Lee, too. It's nice having older brothers. Amen."

"Who do you think might see me?" Lee whispered. His eyes were wide now.

"Don't be scared. You just have to walk ten yards to the shed over there," I said in my most calming voice and pointed to Daddy's work shed behind our house. "Besides, we'll yell if we see anybody coming. Now, go git the shovel and quit askin' so many questions!" Lee was making me impatient.

Lee crawled carefully from under the house. He squatted for a minute to look around. Then he ran to the shed and quickly opened the door. When he disappeared inside, I turned to Richard.

"Richard, are you in or out?" I was excited.

"I'm in." Richard's voice quivered.

Buried treasure was something that didn't just happen too often, especially this far inland from the ocean. Mark had told us bedtime stories about Blackbeard and his pirates who had buried gold and diamonds and silver along the North Carolina coastline. Who knew? Maybe one of the pirates had gotten lost and buried his treasure close to the old oak tree. I hoped we'd find enough treasure to buy presents for everyone. I began making a mental list.

1. Daddy wanted a new floor-sanding machine for his
       business.
2. Mama wanted a new bedspread and curtains for her
       bedroom.
3. We'd give Mark spending money, so he could quit his
       paper job.
4. Mary would get a new dress and maybe even a pair
       of shoes to match.

5. I wanted an official size, real leather football.
6. Lee wanted a new baseball and bat since I'd thrown his other ball down the neighbor's well.
7. Lizzie could use a new baby doll that had some clean clothes.
8. We'd get Tommy a new rattle and some new diapers. All of his cloth diapers were stained - hand-me-downs from when we were little.

"Richard, what do you want when we find the treasure?" I asked.

"I don't know. I guess I'd really like to have my own Bible with pictures, so I don't have to borrow Mama's all the time. A new Shooter might be nice, too, since I'm getting better at marbles."

"I think we'll be able to handle that," I replied with assurance.

Yeah, the treasure would come in handy. I could picture us buying everyone presents—our two grandmothers, our aunts, uncles, cousins, Mrs. Johnson, and even Russell Thomas. We'd be so rich, it would be like Christmas all year round!

Lee carried the large shovel with both hands and stood waiting outside.

"Lizzie. You can't go. You stay here under the house," I ordered. "You'll jest git in the way."

Lizzie's lips puckered out, her bottom lip started to quiver, and the tears began to flow. She started crying really loud.

"Shut her up!" I yelled to Richard. "Mama'll think we did somethin' to her to make her cry."

Lizzie cried even louder.

"Roy, let her go," Richard pleaded. "We can't leave her here. It's too dangerous! I'll take care of Lizzie, myself. Okay?"

Lizzie cried even louder than before. We heard Mama's

footsteps heading towards the front door. It opened.

"Roy, what's wrong with Lizzie?" Mama shouted.

"Nothin. She's okay, aren't you, Lizzie?" I yelled towards the front of the house.

"Well, we'll have lunch ready in a couple of hours. I'll call you when it's ready."

"Okay," I shouted back and turned towards Lizzie. "Lizzie, stop crying. You can go, but you have to stop crying first. We can't let anyone know what we're doing. If you want a new baby doll, you're gonna have to quit crying. Richard, she's your responsibility, and you can't let her git in the way," I said with a warning look.

"She won't. I promise, cross my heart." Richard seemed relieved.

And as easily as Lizzie's tears started, the tears stopped. Lizzie was getting to be a smart girl by learning quickly how to get her way. We crawled out from under the house and cautiously ran down the street towards the red stop sign. I silently prayed that we wouldn't run into the neighborhood bullies. Especially not now with so much at stake. I folded the treasure map and tucked it into one of my worn overall's pockets. According to the treasure map, we were to turn right at the stop sign and go across a weedy area towards the large oak tree we sometimes climbed.

"Look! There's the tree!" Lee pointed. He held Daddy's old shovel in one hand and pointed with the other. Damp hair hung down over his eyes.

"Shush!" I shot back. "Are you tryin to tell the whole world? I know where the tree is. Hey, Richard! Are you two comin' or are you jest gonna stand there?"

"We're comin'," Richard called. "C'mon Lizzie. We have to hurry up."

I began wading through the knee-high weeds towards the clearing around the tree. Lee was close behind me. Richard took Lizzie's little hand and began guiding her through the ocean of weeds towards us.

"Snakes, snakes!" Lizzie whined. I quickly shot Richard an "I told you so" look.

"There are no snakes around here, Lizzie," Richard promised. "Just hold my hand and you'll be okay. See? I'm not scared."

I said a quick prayer that we wouldn't run into any sleeping snakes. One day when Richard, Lee, and I were walking up the road to the stop sign, we saw a long black snake slither across the dirt road in front of us and disappear into the weeds. I hoped he wasn't anywhere close by today.

"Gimme the shovel," I demanded.

"Naw, sir. I went and got the shovel. I carried it all this way, so I'm doin' the diggin'," Lee hissed loudly between clinched teeth.

"Roy, let him do the diggin'. Why don't you read the map and make sure he digs in the right place?" Richard suggested.

"Well, okay. That makes sense." I was satisfied; besides, Lee could do the hard work.

We stood around the tree, looking over our shoulders every chance we got to make sure we hadn't been followed. No one was in sight except for Mrs. Johnson who was sweeping her front porch. Richard waved at her, and she smiled and waved back to him. He visited her everyday while we were at school. He enjoyed her famous chocolate-chip cookies while she told him about her late husband and their grown children. Richard said she mainly told him Bible stories. Of course, he loved that. She even taught him the Ten Commandments.

"Richard. Have you ever heard of the Ten Commandments?"

"Yes, m'am. Thou shalt not kill. Thou shalt not steal. Right?"

"Yes! That's really good. Do you know the other ones?" she asked.

"No, m'am, but I've heard Reverend Small talk about them."

"Well, I'm going to teach all of them to you."

I was proud of my little brother who was the only kid in the neighborhood who knew them all by heart. And while he learned the Ten Commandments over the course of several visits, she fed him lots of chocolate-chip cookies and milk. He even brought us cookies. At night, I'd hear him saying a prayer for her. It was always the same.

"Dear Jesus, please bless Mrs. Johnson and please take care of Mr. Johnson. Mrs. Johnson is really lonely since he's gone."

I turned back to check Lee's progress. Lee had dug two holes and was digging another. He hadn't found anything yet.

"Try over here on the east side of the tree," I instructed him.

"East side? How do you know it's the east side? Where's the east side?"

"I don't know, maybe around here. Anyway, just do it."

Lee started digging again, and it wasn't long before he'd struck something hard. We heard a loud "thump."

"Look, Roy, look!" he squealed with delight. "It's a box! It's a wooden box. I found it! Look Richard! Look Lizzie!" His laughter was contagious. We were all giggling from excitement.

We knelt down on our knees and began pawing at the soft earth. We looked liked dogs unburying bones. I watched an earthworm wiggle around and slither off to bury itself again. Soon, the small wooden box was unearthed. I grabbed the brown container and lifted it from its shallow grave. We all looked around to ensure no one was seeing the treasure box. A cord was wrapped around it twice and neatly tied in a bow to keep the wooden lid on. It seemed a little strange for a pirate to take time to tie a bow, but I didn't saying anything. I untied the bow. Before lifting the lid, I paused and looked into each of the big eyes staring back at me. I took a loud, deep breath and removed the lid. We couldn't believe our eyes! There was a wad of green dollar bills, six packs of gum, six pieces of individually wrapped hard candy, and a big bag of black licorice that just happened to be our favorite candy.

"One, two, three, four, five, six, seven, eight, nine, ten, eleven, twelve, thirteen, fourteen! Fourteen whole dollars! We're rich!" I shouted.

Richard's eyes shone bright with excitement. Lee was smiling broadly. We all were. Lizzie was jumping up and down. I couldn't tell if she had to go to the bathroom or if she was just excited.

"Wow, Roy! We're rich! What are we gonna do with all this money?" Lee asked.

"I don't know, little brother." My whole attitude had certainly changed.

"Richy, I gotta pee pee," Lizzie cried. Her hands were wedged between her crossed legs, and she was bouncing from foot to foot.

"Okay, Lizzie, c'mon." Richard led her to the other side of the tree and behind a bush away from Lee and me.

"Don't forget to pull her pants down, so we don't have any accidents this time," I whispered loudly.

"Man, can you believe this?" Lee asked. "What dopes!"

"What are you talking about?" I asked.

"Here, read this!"

I took a white piece of paper from Lee's extended hand. After reading it, we both fell over onto the ground laughing. The treasure contents spilled out and lay in the weeds beside the empty box.

"What's that?" Richard asked pointing to the white paper.

"Aw nuthin', Richard. It's jest a note from Daddy," I said with a laugh.

"Daddy? Whatdaya mean? Why would there be a note from Daddy with the buried treasure?"

I stopped laughing, sat up on one elbow and wiped my eyes. I read the note aloud.

"Hope you've had fun finding buried treasure. Share everything – the candy and gum with your other brothers and sisters. Remember that Tommy is too young for candy and gum, but save his money so when he's old enough, he can spend it himself. Love, Daddy."

"Wow. Whadda ya think has gotten into Daddy?" Lee asked. "He never gives us money for no reason."

"I don't know," I replied with a frown. I was puzzled.

"Maybe it's just because he loves us," Richard said quietly.

Lee and I stared at Richard for a long time like it was a new idea we'd never considered. Then, I shrugged my shoulders and smiled at Richard.

"Yeah, I guess that's it. Richard, why don't you keep Tommy's dollars for him? You know me. I'll accidentally spend them if I do, and I don't trust Lee," I teased.

"What do ya mean by that?" Lee asked.

"Just jokin," I said. "Here's yours and Tommy's share, Richard. Lee, here's yours. I've got Mark's and Mary's. Lizzie, do you want Richard to hold yours, or will you lose it?"

"Richy. I want my candy! I want my candy!" She cried.

Lizzie could have cared less about the money. She had no idea how much candy two dollars could buy. I passed out the candy, picked up the wooden box, and we headed home. I remember when I stuffed my two dollars in my pocket, a strange feeling washed over my whole body. A knot tightened in the middle of my stomach. Richard was right. Daddy did love us. But he'd been sick for a long time. Was he afraid that he wasn't getting better? I didn't want to think about it.

We ran home for lunch and told Mama all about the treasure.

"Isn't that just like your daddy?" she smiled.

Mary grabbed her two dollars and candy and just

squealed. "Let's meet Daddy this afternoon at the stop sign. Let's be there to surprise him and to say thank you."

"Good idea!" I answered. Too bad I hadn't thought of that.

Usually, I was the only one who met Daddy's work truck each afternoon, but he deserved something different today.

Right on time, Daddy turned his floor-sanding work truck off the paved road and slowly onto our dirt street. Mark was sitting on the passenger's side. Even though Daddy looked really tired, he immediately flashed us a big toothy smile when he saw all of us standing there with our mouths stuffed with gum. He stopped the truck for us to hop onto the truck bed and sit among the floor sanding equipment. In between dry coughs, he was whistling his favorite song, "My Wild Irish Rose." As he inched down the street, he proudly tipped his hat to Mrs. Johnson who sat in a rocking chair on her front porch. He waved at Russell Thomas' dad who was trimming hedges. When he parked the truck in our driveway, he climbed down and slowly made his way to the back of the vehicle. He started to laugh as we blew bubbles with the gum, but that was quickly replaced by another coughing spasm. He pulled out a stained handkerchief and covered his cracked lips.

"Looks like you found some buried treasure today."

He barely got the words out before he started coughing again. This time he coughed for a long time before it finally, mercifully, stopped. He tried to pick Richard up, but he couldn't, so he began tickling him under the armpits instead – Richard's most sensitive spot. I remember I started crying. At the time, I thought I was crying because I was laughing hard at Richard's gleeful laughter. Daddy ruffled Lee's and my hair.

"Where's my baby girl?" he asked as he slowly swung Lizzie onto his shoulders. This familiar gesture seemed to take a lot of effort.

Mary hugged Daddy around his waist, while Mark observed with a serious look on his face. How we loved our father!

"Thanks, Daddy!" We all exclaimed in unison.

He looked long and hard at each one of us. Then, he walked up the short porch steps and into the house to kiss Mama hello. We heard him singing "My Wild Irish Rose" in his weakened voice.

That night at the supper table, the coughing began again. The white handkerchief used to cover his mouth quickly changed to crimson. To this day, I don't like the color red because I saw it once too often. We watched in horror as our father's life oozed out of his mouth between his cracked lips and left its stain on the handkerchief. Each cough shook his slender body from head to foot. Resigned that he couldn't eat his food, he left the table.

"I'm sorry," he apologized with watery eyes.

We were sorry, too. For him and for us.

Chapter 14

You will go out in joy and be led forth in peace; the mountains and hills will burst into song before you, and all the trees of the field will clap their hands.
Isaiah 55: 12

Richard: On one particular summer's evening when supper was eaten and the dishes were washed, I remember Mama and Daddy passed the night away sitting on the porch steps watching us run around our grassy backyard. They held hands and shared the day's activities in low voices. Mark and Mary were playing "Red Rover," "Mother May I?" and "Hide-n-Seek" with us. Our excited squeals and gleeful yells had attracted several of the neighborhood kids to join in the fun. On nights like these, I felt like I could burst with happiness. We were all together, safe and sound, complete. Everything was all right. After the sun disappeared behind the trees, the moon quickly stepped in to take over.

Once, Granny had told me a story that I thought of on nights like these.

"At the end of the day," she'd say, "the sun goes down and sleeps while the moon takes over the duties of providing light for Mother Earth. But the moon needs help because it isn't able to provide the same bright light as the sun. So God had a solution. He created little night bugs to flitter carelessly here and there."

"I've seen them, Granny! I've seen them!" I cried.

"Of course you have, Richard. And he told his angels to tie little lanterns to their tails, so the bugs could see where they were flying in the dark. We call these tiny creatures fireflies or lightning bugs."

Roy, Lee, Mary, and I found these little creatures fascinating. So much so that they were worthy of being captured and placed in empty mason jars. On this late June night, we each carefully prepared our little glass prisons beforehand by adding little pieces of wet grass and other summer flowers so the prisoners would have moisture and drinking water. Daddy created air holes by puncturing the lids with an ice pick.

"Why do you children have to catch those poor little bugs?" Mama asked.

"We're not going to hurt them, Mama," I reassured her.

"Tell that to the lightning bugs," she replied while shaking her head.

"Let them be," Daddy laughed. "Besides, I bet you caught lightning bugs when you were a little girl."

"I did a lot of things when I was a little girl," Mama chuckled. "But I've learned a lot since then."

"They're just kids having fun. Just sit here with me and watch them." Then he shouted, "Whose gonna catch the most lightning bugs?" His shout brought on another coughing spell. We stopped what we were doing and patiently waited for it to stop.

"I am," Roy replied, breaking our silence.

"No, I will," Lee shouted.

"Me want to catch light bugs, too," Lizzie whined.

"C'mon Lizzie. You help me. Me and Lizzie will," I cried. This was going to be fun.

"Richy, I want to hold the jar. Lemme hold the jar, Richy."

"Okay, but don't drop it," I warned.

How funny we must have looked running around in circles or zigzagging with our jars clutched tightly by one hand and reaching high into the air to capture the tiny lights. We didn't care! This was summer fun at its best!

Unfortunately, even summer nights end and there is no escaping the time the clock tells.

"Okay, kids. Let's call it a night. Mark and I have to go to work in the morning," Daddy called. When Daddy spoke, you'd better listen, because he gave few second chances.

Reluctantly, we ended another precious summer day

and night. Before climbing into bed, Mama and Daddy followed us into our room, so Daddy could count the bugs in our jars and declare a winner. On this particular night, Lee had caught the most.

"Looks like Roy has eight. Richard, you have seven. Let's see, Lee. One-two-three-four-five-six-seven-eight-nine-ten. Ten! You have ten, so it looks like you're the winner, tonight." Daddy went over and ruffled Lee's hair. Lee just grinned. "In the morning, I expect you to let them all go, okay, boys? Besides, if you let 'em go, then you can catch 'em again tomorrow night."

"Yes, sir," we all replied in unison.

"Mark, I'll wake you up in the morning."

"Okay, Dad. Goodnight."

Goodnight, boys. Sleep tight."

"Night, Daddy. Night, Mama."

"Night."

Yes. We'd let the bugs go in the morning, but tonight they belonged to us. With heavy eyelids, we watched the occasional flickers of tiny lights. Finally, these calming lights lulled us into a deep sleep.

****

"Lee! Over here! Over here!" I laughed. "There are a lot of them over here!"

"I'm coming. Reach out and grab them before they get away. Reach out!" Lee cried.

"I am. Isn't this fun?" I asked.

"Yeah. It's the greatest," Lee yelled.

"Richard! Lee! What are you two doing?" Mark called from a distance. His voice interrupted our play. I couldn't concentrate. He was getting closer and closer, louder and louder.

"Richard! Lee! Wake up. Wake up!" Mark seemed like he was yelling.

I rubbed my groggy eyes with my closed fists, tried to focus in the dark, and turned towards the familiar voice. Mark was standing barefoot in the middle of the bedroom with a puzzled look on his face. Roy was sitting up with a weird look on his face, too. I wasn't running around in the middle of our backyard catching lightning bugs. I was in our bedroom, and Lee was standing in the corner of the room next to the dresser. He was swatting the air with his hands. How did we get in here so quickly?

"Lee. Lee," Mark called gently as he placed his hands firmly on Lee's back. "Wake up, Lee." Mark guided Lee back to the bed he shared with Roy. Lee didn't say anything. He just climbed into bed and closed his eyes again.

I slid beneath the wrinkled cotton sheets beside Mark and waited. I was perplexed and afraid that Mark was going to be mad at me.

"Are you okay?" Roy asked from across the room. "Were you asleep, or were you two playing like it?"

"I think I was asleep. I don't know about Lee. This is weird. I thought we were outside catching lightning bugs. And that's the honest truth, cross my heart and hope to live."

"Uh-huh," Roy replied with a skeptical look. "Go to sleep, safari hunter."

"Okay, now. Hush. Let's get some sleep," Mark said. "I have to go to work in a few hours."

If Lee ever remembered the dream of catching lightning bugs that night, he never owned up to it. But it was neat to know that my brother and I had shared the same dream.

Chapter 15

Those who bring sunshine to the lives of others cannot keep it from themselves.
James M. Barrie

Roy: On Saturday mornings, we used to take turns going with Daddy downtown to pay bills, like the electric bill or the telephone bill, or to run other errands that he hadn't been able to do during the week. He always liked to walk through the Sears and Roebuck store before ending up at the barbershop where he'd get his bi-weekly haircut.

I liked going to Sears, too, because my nose always led me in the direction of the candy counter where special chocolates were displayed on white, doily-draped shelves behind sparkling clean glass windows. Freshly-popped popcorn and all kinds of expensive nuts filled other glass bins. The aromas were hard for anyone to ignore, and it was easy for me to persuade Daddy to buy a bag of delectable chocolates to share with my siblings. Occasionally, he even indulged and bought himself a treat – a pound of warm cashews.

The last Saturday trip we spent together is a favorite memory for lots of reasons. I happily walked beside Daddy clutching a precious bag of chocolates tightly in my hand. Another coughing spell had caused him to lose any interest in buying cashew nuts. Up and down the aisles of the hardware department, we slowly sauntered until we stood in front of the saltwater fishing supplies. I noticed that Daddy didn't walk as fast as he used to. He had a coughing spasm and grabbed a nearby shelf for support.

"Daddy, are you okay?" I asked. His frequent coughing scared me.

"I'm all right." He tried to reassure me with a smile.

Afterwards, I watched him study the various tackle boxes and saltwater reels. I became bored, so I turned around to look at something different. That's when I saw it. It was beautiful! It had to be the most beautiful blue bicycle I'd ever seen.

The fenders were silver chrome that glistened under the store's overhead lights. The handlebars had blue rubber handles on each end, and in the exact center, there was a single headlight. On top of the back bumper was a chrome rack that could serve as a seat or as a carrying compartment. The bike's 24-inch frame was positioned on two wide black and white-walled tires. I was entranced!

Daddy broke the silence. "What are you looking at?"

"Isn't it a beaut? Wow. I'd love to have a bike like this."

"You would? But you have a bike."

"Yeah, one that I share with Mark and Lee."

"Well, with Mark working now, he probably won't be using the bike very often. So that means you only have to share it with Lee, right?"

"Right."

He ruffled my hair. "Let's go home. Mama's probably worried about us."

For the next week, I just couldn't erase the bicycle from my mind. I had never wanted anything so much in my short lifetime. Christmas was several months away—almost an eternity! The old bicycle that Mark, Lee, and I shared was blue, plain, and beat up from lots of wear and tear. We needed a new bike; I needed a new bike, but how would I ever convince Mama and Daddy? I lost several nights of sleep from tossing and turning and creating all kinds of convincing stories in my mind. Then it came to me! Why had it taken so long to think of something so easy? With my new plan well thought-out, I started taking the actions necessary to get the new bike.

Richard had just turned six in May, but he seemed more than content to ride a tricycle for the rest of his life. I would put a stop to that. Why, I was riding the bicycle by the time I was five years old and without training wheels. Besides, we didn't have the training wheels that had come with it. Maybe if I taught Richard how to ride a bike, then Daddy would understand that four or even three boys couldn't possibly share one bicycle. Mark and I could share the new bike, and Lee and Richard could share the older bike. Besides, Daddy was right! Mark didn't ride a bike anymore since he had a part-time job. This meant I'd have the new bike all to myself.

"Come on, Richard. I'm gonna teach you how to ride a bike," I said smiling my sweetest smile.

"Naw. That's okay," Richard stammered, shaking his head back and forth.

"Don't you want to learn how to ride?" I asked while standing beside the bike and offering the handle-bars to him.

"Not really," he replied.

"Why not?" My voice was rising.

"I'm okay not riding anything. Besides, I can still ride the tricycle."

I knew this wasn't going to be easy. Nothing in my life was ever easy. But I was determined to have a new bicycle, and no little brother was going to stand in the way of my plan. I watched him throw a rock into the middle of the street. I'd have to try a different approach.

"You're too big to ride a tricycle. You look silly. You're six years old. Do ya want people to start thinking you're sissy? I was ridin' a bike without training wheels when I was younger than you. Besides, it's really easy. I'll learn ya in no time at all."

"No Roy. Just leave me alone. I don't want to learn how to ride." Of course he didn't. That would make my life too easy.

"Why not, Richard?" I pleaded.

"I just don't."

"You and Lee can have the bicycle when you learn how to ride."

"What?"

"You and Lee can have the bicycle all to yourselves when you learn how to ride."

"What will you ride, Roy? That wouldn't be fair to you."

"I don't know. I guess I'll do without." I hung my head in my most convincing martyr's way. "C'mon, Richard. Besides, it will make Mama and Daddy really proud of you. If I can do it, you can do it. Remember, you're a lot smarter than me."

"Well, okay, then." He was gullible.

"Let's go in the backyard where there's grass in case you fall. You'll scratch your knees in the dirt if you fall here."

"Fall?" His eyes were big.

"You're not going to fall. I'll hold you up until you get the hang of it." I had to be more careful with my choice of words.

"You promise me, Roy?" His eyes were inquisitive and scared.

"I promise." I held up my hand in a scout's promise even though I wasn't a Scout.

We walked to the sloping backyard that was green with grass. I held the two-wheeler steady as he climbed onto the bicycle's vacant black seat. The sole of his foot laid flat on the bottom pedal. This would be a cinch! I'd have him riding a bike in no time at all. All it took was a good teacher and someone as determined as me.

"It's just like riding the tricycle. Hold the handlebars and pedal. That's all you have to do."

"Okay, but don't let go," he pleaded.

"Okay, I won't let go," I replied impatiently.

Four times he pedaled the bike down the short hill while I ran beside him holding the seat with one hand and the handlebars with the other. When we got to the end of the yard, we turned around and returned the bike to its starting point. He actually was enjoying this. That is, until the fifth time when I released the handlebars and he panicked.

"Don't let go. You promised," Richard reminded me.

"I'm still holding onto the seat, Richard. I'm not going

to let you fall."

I jogged beside the bike with just one hand on the seat to steady him. He turned his head backwards to watch me. The handlebars turned quickly, and the bike toppled over. Richard looked like he'd start crying any minute.

"You're okay. C'mon and don't cry." I tried hard to soothe him.

After a few minutes, he quieted down. "I don't wanna do it anymore."

"Sure you do. You've almost got it. You're doing really good." The vision of the new bicycle was dancing before my eyes. It was within my grasp.

Finally, I convinced him to climb onto the seat again. We steered the bike so it was heading down the sloping yard. Several times, he pedaled while I ran along beside him. Once he had regained his confidence, it was time to let go. We returned the bike to its original position without my normal promise. (My fingers were crossed.) I pushed the bike and yelled for him to pedal. Richard traveled for about ten feet before falling onto the cool green grass. This time he didn't cry. We were both determined. I pushed him down the hill over and over again. Then it happened! The bicycle remained upright as he pedaled to the end of the yard. We were both ecstatic! Richard's eyes were dancing and were almost as bright as his big smile. Richard was riding a bicycle, and I'd taught him! This was the most exciting thing I'd ever done. My little brother could ride a bike! I was so proud of him.

After telling Mama, we ran to the stop sign and waited for Daddy's truck that afternoon. We couldn't wait to tell him the news. Later, I found myself standing between my parents while the three of us watched my little brother reach a childhood milestone. The snaggletooth smile on his face was spread from ear to ear. He was beaming with excitement and pride. We all were.

The next afternoon, I ran outside to play after supper. The blue bicycle wasn't leaning against the side of the house.

Then I heard laughter. Richard was happily pedaling the bike around the house and down the backyard with Lee running after him.

"Can I ride the bicycle?" I yelled smiling.

"Nope!" Lee yelled. "Besides, you gave the bike to me and Richard. But you can ride the tricycle." His remark was not funny, and his happiness definitely was not contagious.

Two afternoons later, Daddy got off work early to take me to Sears and Roebuck to buy the new J.C. Higgins blue and silver-chromed bicycle with a headlight.

"You deserve it, Roy. You taught your brother how to ride knowing that three of you would be sharing a bike. Besides, maybe two bikes will make things easier. Maybe I can buy another bike in a few weeks. Then you won't have to share at all."

I wasn't really listening to what Daddy was saying. I couldn't wait to get the "beaut" home. Russell Thomas would be so jealous!

"Gee, Daddy. Thanks! This is the bestest present I ever got. Today's better than Christmas!"

"Yeah. It's a nice bike. C'mon. Let's get home before your mother calls the sheriff." Between short, irritating coughs, he laughed. I laughed. Then he ruffled my hair.

I remembering him standing in the driveway that evening, proudly watching me ride up and down the street until it was dark. He said he wanted to be sure the chrome headlight worked.

Chapter 16

*For none of us lives to himself alone and none of us dies to himself
alone. If we live, we live to the Lord; and if we die, we die to the Lord.
So, whether we live or die, we belong to the Lord.*
Romans 14: 7-8

Richard: At the beginning of July, Daddy admitted himself into
the sanitarium. Our visits were limited since tuberculosis, or
T.B. as it was called, was such a dreadful and contagious disease. On my last visit to see Daddy, I heard Miss Jacobs, the
head nurse, whispering to Mama. She told her that eighty-five
percent of those who had T.B. never recovered with complete
bed rest being the only hope. Unfortunately, antibiotics were
not invented when Daddy needed them.

On my last visit to see Daddy, he was wearing the reas-
suring smile that I had grown to expect and love. He talked
to me in his weakened voice, interrupted by the inevitable
coughing spasms. The red blood that appeared at the corners
of his lips was the most frightening thing to me.

Mama and Miss Jacobs came over to his bedside.
Mama held his hand and kissed his forehead, while Miss Jacobs poured ice water from a glass pitcher into a paper cup
and handed it to him.

"Richard, tell Miss Jacobs what you want to be when
you grow up," he gasped after drinking a sip of water.

"I want to be a preacher when I grow up," I enthusias-
tically stated.

Mama and Daddy smiled at each other.

"And why is that, young man?" The stern lady asked.
She was dressed in all white from her head to her toes.

"Well, it's because I like goin' to church with Mama and
hearin' about all the different Bible stories. Maybe one day, I
can even preach like Reverend Small."

"That's nice!" she replied. Then, she looked at Daddy.
"I'm going to get the thermometer. It's time to take your tem-

perature. I'll be right back."

"Yeah? Well, take your time." Daddy wheezed.

"Randall! Behave yourself." Mama was laughing. "That wasn't nice. Here. Raise up and let me fluff your pillows."

"I don't need my pillows fluffed. Besides, she wouldn't know what to do if I acted any different." Then he weakly rolled his head towards me.

"Hey, Richard, that's good. <Cough> That's a good thing for you <Cough> to want to be. I hope you do become a preacher. Just remember this. <Cough> Remember what your daddy's saying, <Cough> okay?"

"Yes, sir."

With effort, he turned onto his left side, slowly raised up on his left elbow, and said, "You can do anything you want to do in this world if you try hard enough. <Cough> You can become anything <Cough> you want to be. Don't ever <Cough> let anyone <Cough> tell you different, understand? <Cough> I will be so proud of you if you <Cough> become a preacher if that's what you want to be <Cough>. I'll be proud of you if you become a floor sander <Cough> or a truck <Cough> driver or <Cough> a teacher. You make me proud just being you. <Cough> I want you to know that and always remember it. You're a special little boy. <Cough> <Cough> Yes sir – a special little boy. I love you, son." <Cough>

On my last visit to see Daddy, I started crying and buried my head in his stomach. "I love you, too, Daddy. Everyday, I pray for you to get better. I pray a lot about it, too."

"I know you do. <Cough>. I know you have been praying for me. You're <Cough> a good boy. Just remember that <Cough> sometimes the prayers we ask for are not always answered the way we want them to be <Cough>."

"Why not?" I asked. I didn't understand. Didn't God answer our prayers like the Bible said he did? "The Bible says that our prayers are heard and answered."

"I know. Prayers are always answered, but <Cough> just not always the way we think they <Cough> should be."

"Randall, quit talking so much," Mama warned him.

"I'm talking to my boy. Richard, you keep those prayers coming for me. <Cough> <Cough> But no matter what happens, <Cough> I'll always love you, and I'll always be with you, Mama, and your brothers and sisters. <Cough> Tell them that for me, will you? Always make sure they know I told you that. Promise me." Then he stopped smiling. A tear trickled down his cheek before he started coughing again.

Mama was crying, too.

"I promise, Daddy. I promise. I will." I tried to return his smile, but I couldn't. I thought my heart was going to break into. Something bad was going to happen, and it didn't seem like there was any way of stopping it. Even though I couldn't fully understand the impact of his words that day, I was able to remember them. His precious words were a comfort to me for the rest of my life.

****

So after Daddy died and the men in black suits closed the coffin lid for the last time, I knew my daddy was hovering close by, watching over us, and keeping us safe. I could just picture him with beautiful angel's wings and a golden halo over his head, just like the pictures in Mama's Bible. Surely, Daddy loved us as he'd always loved us. But now, he loved us from afar.

Post-Event Life

Chapter 17

It is one of the most beautiful compensations of life that no man can sincerely try to help another without helping himself.
Ralph Waldo Emerson

Roy: The next few weeks are a blur in my memory. Somehow, we managed to return to school the next Monday; that is, everyone except Mark. He had decided he was not going back to high school even though he hadn't yet completed his first day. I was standing in the doorway listening to his one-sided conversation with Mama.

"But, Mama, I'm the eldest and that makes me the man of the house, now. That also means that I've got to become the primary bread-winner."

Mama sat on the edge of the kitchen chair, clasping a cooled cup of coffee with both hands. She stared blankly in his direction. At first, I didn't think she was listening, but momentarily, she shrugged her shoulders and nodded slowly in agreement.

"All right. If you think that's what you want to do."

When Mark left the kitchen, I cornered him. "You just can't stop goin' to school, Mark. Daddy wanted all of us to have an education. Remember?"

"Just stay out of this Roy. Besides, Daddy's gone. We have to eat, don't we?" Mark's voice was low and steady, but it had a warning tone. He cut his eyes in my direction and said a little softer,"I know what I'm doing. Trust me. That's all I ask. I've talked with Mr. Critcher, and I can keep my part-time job selling newspapers. After I finish selling papers, I'll work with Uncle Russ in the business. He says I'm a natural, just like Daddy. Uncle Russ will give me a ride to work and bring me home in the afternoons. It's all worked out; there's nothing to worry about. I'll be fine. More importantly, we'll be fine." He brushed by me to ruffle my hair. I dodged his hand.

"You're not Daddy," I grimaced.

"I know that quite well. You don't need to remind me."

Mark was my big brother and my hero. Out of admiration, I tried hard to be like him, but his shoes were hard to fill. Looking back, I don't know if I ever told him how much I appreciated his willingness to sacrifice for us.

That first Monday, the wind-up clock's annoying chime woke me from a restless sleep. Richard jumped up and pressed the ringer. Merciful silence! We all dressed quickly into our designated school clothes. Mary prepared our breakfast of oatmeal and ice water. We didn't have any milk to drink since it was spoiled. Until now, we'd always had juice – grape, apple, orange, or my favorite, grapefruit, because Daddy believed in us having our daily supply of Vitamin C. Since Mama hadn't bought groceries in a week, the refrigerator was almost empty, and we'd eaten up all the food people had brought to the house when Daddy died. Actually, we'd gotten tired of eating it and had thrown a lot of it out. Lee and I washed the dishes while Mary gave Tommy his morning bottle. Afterwards, we grabbed our notebooks, brown paper sacks, each stuffed with a cheese sandwich and an apple for lunch, and headed outside to wait on the front porch for the school bus. Mark joined us there while Mary changed Tommy's diaper and put him back in his crib.

It was difficult to watch Uncle Russ driving Daddy's black truck slowly down the street towards our house to get Mark. The white lettering, "Randall's Flooring Company," was vividly painted on both side doors. My breath quickened, so I closed my eyes tight and wished with all my strength that when I opened my eyes again, I'd see Daddy sitting behind the steering wheel of the old truck. He'd be smiling and singing "My Wild Irish Rose" just like he always did. This past week would have been a bad dream – a nightmare that I'd had. Needless to say, when I opened my eyes, I was disappointed. Then I remembered Daddy's bloody coughing spasms, and I felt a sense of relief that they were over for him, and for us.

Out of the corner of my eye, I watched everyone's face as the beloved pick-up truck turned into our driveway. I'm sure we all shared the same wish, the same poignant memory.

"Hey kids!" Uncle Russ beamed. "Ready for school?"

I'm sure Uncle Russ had good intentions, but did he realize why we weren't returning his smile or answering his question? If so, he kept that same genuine smile on his face.

Uncle Russ hopped out from the driver's side of the Ford and tossed each of us a stick of Clark's Teaberry Gum, the one with the advertisement that claimed, "Deliciously different, Teaberry Gum. For that mountain-grown teaberry flavor is refreshingly cool...juicy...exhilarating!" And it was.

He hurried past us, ruffling our hair as he went, to open the front door. "Mark, go ahead and get in the truck. I'm just gonna say hello to Iris and get a quick cup of coffee."

Before any of us could stop him, he yelled, "Iris? Got a cup of coffee?"

We followed his march through the house where at last he found Mama lying in bed where she'd begun staying the past few days.

"Iris? Are you sick? Is something wrong?"

She was staring up at the plain white ceiling through red-rimmed eyes. She was oblivious to his close proximity, just lying there while the minutes of her life ticked slowly by. Lizzie was asleep, snuggled next to Mama and curled in a fetal position with her right thumb stuck securely in her mouth. She was too young to dote on sadness and too young to have worries—no chores, no school, no homework, no bullies, no Daddy, nothing. I suddenly felt jealous of Lizzie. This emotion joined my other ambiguous feelings of confusion, sadness, grief, and anger.

During the latter part of the week, Lizzie had begun having nightmares. Night after night, she had awakened crying, "Daddy! Daddy! Please hold Lizzie. Daddy, pick me up. Pick me up." Of course, her crying awoke Tommy who cried his lungs out. Mama didn't even seem to notice or even hear all of the commotion. She never came into Lizzie and Mary's bedroom to comfort her crying daughter, so Mary had to. The rest of us took turns rocking Tommy back to sleep.

Those three or four nights were some of the longest ones in my life, just sitting there with my brothers in the shadows of our living room with one of us rocking Tommy back to sleep. Sometimes, I could picture the coffin sitting in the middle of the room with people tiptoeing around it as if Daddy could be disturbed. I found myself mumbling prayers for Tommy to hurry back to sleep, so we could get out of this room and back into the comforts of our own beds. By Sunday morning, we all looked like walking zombies. Mama must have noticed our dark rimmed eyes and lack of energy when she shuffled into the kitchen in her pink bathrobe to fix a cup of coffee for herself. She looked around the table at all of us while we sat silently eating dry toast and grape jelly. We were out of butter.

"Lizzie can sleep with me for a while, at least until these nightmares stop. You all need to get your sleep especially when you go back to school tomorrow. You look tired. I'm sorry I haven't been much help these past few days."

Luckily, the nightmares stopped. Over the next few weeks, we found ourselves standing beside Mama's bed every morning, saying goodbye before leaving for school. One of us would cough, usually me, to interrupt her blank stare and to draw her attention to our presence. Each morning, Mary knelt beside the double bed and gently rubbed Mama's hands or finger-brushed her black hair from her perspiring forehead. This became our morning ritual.

"Mama, we're gettin' ready to go to school. I've fed Tommy, changed his diaper, and put him back in his crib. He's playin' right now. Do you need anything before we leave?" Mary asked sweetly.

No answer.

Mary continued, "Well, he'll go back to sleep in a little while. The boys washed the breakfast dishes. If you don't need anything, then we're going."

Finally, Mama would come out of her daze and recite a memorized litany in her newly acquired monotone voice. "No – I'll be all right. Thank you. You're good children. You kids be good today in school, and study hard. Learn a lot, and I'll see you when you get home."

Then we took turns giving her kisses and hugs and telling her goodbye. We'd leave Mama's bedside to gather our notebooks, textbooks and pencil boxes. We'd grab our wrinkled, brown-paper sacks that contained peanut butter crackers or peanut butter sandwiches and an apple or pear prepared the night before by Mary.

After several days of our new ritual, I began wondering why she even bothered saying anything to us at all. She certainly didn't mean it. We could have written her meaningless words on a piece of paper and hung it over her bed. It would have meant just as much to us as her memorized litany meant now. And after a few more days, I wondered why we even bothered going into her room to say goodbye.

On another morning, I noticed Richard had deliberately remained behind after Mary and Lee left for the bus stop. I stood quietly in the living room and curiously eavesdropped as Richard whispered to our mother.

"Mama, everythin's gonna be all right. Okay? I'm gonna draw you a real purty pi'ture today in school. We can hang it on the wall over there beside the dresser so you can see it. You're gonna like it. I know you will."

When Mama didn't respond audibly, I heard Richard continue. "I love you, Mama. Don't you worry about anythin'. We're gonna take real good care of you now 'cause Daddy would want us to. Remember, he's an angel with wings who watches over us. Remember? Bye now!" Again, I heard no reply, but his hurried footsteps were coming towards me, so I acted like I'd just opened the front door to leave.

"Ready for school?" I asked.

"Yep! Ready! Let's go!" Richard replied.

I silently pondered what I'd heard as I strolled to the bus stop with Richard. The angry red stop sign stood there reminding me that the majority of our lives were lived within a sad house that stood within its stubborn boundaries. School seemed our only parole.

Chapter 18

When I was a child, I talked like a child, I thought like a child, I reasoned like a child. When I became an adult, I put childish ways behind me.
I Corinthians 13:11

Richard: I didn't know how to ask any of my brothers, but I just had to know if it were true. Mama wasn't exactly acting like herself these days. Mark wouldn't be at home when school was over, Roy's temper would probably get the best of him, and Lee probably didn't know the truth either. So, with some hesitation, I decided to ask Mary.

Quietly, I tiptoed into Mary's pink bedroom where she sat propped up against fluffy pillows doing arithmetic homework. I gently sat down on the end of her bed, so I wouldn't disturb her.

"Hey, Richard. What's up?" Mary asked without looking up.

"How did you know it was me?" Mary was amazing!

"Because. Roy and Lee never walk quietly into any room. Lizzie is napping, Tommy can't walk, and Mark is at work. I guess that leaves you!"

"Oh! That makes sense, Mary," I started saying innocently. "I need to ask you somethin'."

"What? Do you need help with your reading? I used to like the 'Dick, Jane and Spot' stories."

"No. That's not it," I stated in a low voice.

"Then what? You can ask me anything," she reassured me.

She'd stopped writing and was staring at me with a sweet smile.

"Mary, is there such a thing as Santa Claus?"

Mary raised her eyebrows and scratched the side of her nose. She looked down at her notebook and began writing numbers again. "Of course there is. Why are you asking?"

"Well, Mrs. Johns told her class that there is no Santa Claus or Easter Bunny or Tooth Fairy."

"Who is Mrs. Johns?" Mary asked. Actually, Mary demanded. Her voice was rising.

"She's Danny's teacher."

"Who is Danny?"

"He's my friend that rides my school bus. He sat with me this afternoon and told me what Mrs. Johns told his class. She said they were in the first grade, and it was time for them to know the truth."

"What truth?" Mary was acting coy.

"She said no one in her class better act like they believed in Santa Claus anymore. She said they should go home and ask their parents to tell them the truth."

"Oh, she did, did she?" Mary asked slowly. Her voice was shaking. There was plenty of expression coming from her dark eyes. I could tell she wasn't happy about something. She peered straight through me and was talking to some invisible person behind me. As she talked, she got angrier. "What's wrong with that woman? Who does she think she is?"

"Maybe I shouldn't have said anything," I whispered and slid off the bed to escape.

"Oh, yes you should have said something. Mrs. Johns is the one who shouldn't have said anything. Sit down, Richard." Mary patted her bed and smiled at me. She had calmed down.

"Here's the truth. As long as you believe there is a Santa Claus, then I promise you there is one. Really! That's the same for the Easter Bunny and the Tooth Fairy, too. Santa Claus, the Easter Bunny, and the Tooth Fairy come to visit you because you are loved, Richard, and most importantly, because you believe they are true. As long as you believe, they are real. That's what's so special about being a child and seeing the world through a child's eyes. So promise me you'll forget about what Mrs. Johns told her class. Will you do that? Will you believe what I told you? Promise?"

"I promise," I murmured.

"Good! And Richard, it's really not fair to talk to other kids about these kinds of things. Let's keep this a secret for now, so promise you won't talk to Danny or any of the other kids about it."

"What if they bring it up?" I was concerned that this would be the topic of conversation again on the morning ride to school just like it had been the topic this afternoon.

"If they do, just walk away or tell them you'd rather talk about something different," Mary instructed.

"Okay. I guess I can do that. I promise."

"Good, Richard. Just always remember how special you are and what a special time of your life this is. As long as you believe, all kinds of good things will come true."

"Okay, Mary. Thanks!" I walked over to her and kissed her cheek. She grabbed me quickly and hugged me hard.

"Don't forget. You can always talk to me about anything. "Deal?"

"Deal."

As I left my sister's room and entered my own, I knew in my heart of hearts that Mrs. Johns was probably telling the truth, and Mary didn't want me to be disappointed. I wanted the rest of my childhood to be as unblemished and innocent as possible. Two of the people I trusted most in the world were my Mama and Daddy. Their gifts of childhood beliefs that wove the fabrics of imagination and creativity were given out of quintessential love. Now, with Daddy gone and Mama not acting like herself, I was scared I would discover the truth anyway – the hard way. I was scared the Easter Bunny and Santa Claus and the Tooth Fairy wouldn't ever come to visit us again. I was scared they had died the same day my daddy had died. I hoped against hope I was wrong.

Secretly, so did Mary.

Chapter 19

The word impossible is not in my dictionary.
Napoleon Bonaparte

Roy: Each school morning, our neighbor, Mrs. Johnson, slowly waddled across the dirt street to meet us at the stop sign. Her smiling, wrinkled face became the brightest part of our mornings. She never knew how much we appreciated her, and neither did we at the time.

"Open your lunch bags, children. I baked a batch of chocolate-chip cookies last night. Now, promise you won't eat these until lunchtime."

Eagerly, we'd open our meager lunch sacks, and allow her to fill our bags with the homemade treats. Mrs Johnson made delicious homemade oatmeal and raisin cookies, too. Boy, could she cook!

"Roy, honey, your sack is getting really crumpled and dirty. It's time for a new one, isn't it sweetheart?" She really didn't want an answer from me, so I allowed her to continue her monologue. "Mary, you are looking tired, sweetheart. You need some roses in those pretty cheeks of yours. Try to get more sleep at night. Lee! Why your bag is worse than Roy's! Come by my house this afternoon, and I'll give you new sacks for your lunches. There now, did everyone get a cookie?" Mrs. Johnson even gave the bullies on our street cookies.

"Russell, you're looking well today. Can you come by this afternoon and get some boxes down from my attic for me?"

"Yes, ma'am. I'll be more than happy to do that for you. After all, look at what you do for us." Russell turned away and gave me a sly look. You would have thought he was a choirboy in church. I knew better. Poor Mrs. Johnson didn't.

"Richard, did you practice your writing last night?" She acted like a mother hen with all her little chicks gathered around her.

"Don't forget, you have to practice forming your letters

to have good penmanship. Practice makes perfect."

Mrs. Johnson was a good and kind woman without a prejudiced or judgmental bone in her body. Her homemade cookies were a welcome addition to the saltine crackers and peanut butter sandwiches that were becoming the norm and were becoming more unappetizing and dreaded each day. I silently prayed that she'd keep on baking cookies, preferably oatmeal and raisin, every now and then. So far, my prayers had been answered. Mama used to bake us sugar cookies at least once a week, but she hadn't baked anything lately.

Most afternoons, we returned home from school to find Mama still dressed in a faded blue nightgown or her pink bathrobe, asleep on the couch. Lizzie would be sitting on the dusty living room floor amongst a heap of strewn toys. The kitchen sink would be overflowing with empty baby bottles and a few dishes from their meager lunches. And from the acrid smell that greeted us, Tommy would be ready for a diaper change – way past due for one. Over and over again, I read Mary and Richard's disappointment. They were the optimists of the family, hoping that soon we'd find Mama dressed and smiling and the house clean and spotless like it used to be. Lee's eternal smile had begun to fade. He'd shrug his shoulders and slip into our room to do his homework.

Me? I just seemed to get angrier and angrier as the days went by. This wasn't fair! Life wasn't fair! Why didn't Mama get up and cook our breakfast anymore? I was tired of eating cold cereal or oatmeal and drinking water. Why didn't Mama ever get dressed and clean the house? I was tired of seeing her in a gown and bathrobe when I left in the morning and when I returned in the afternoon. Why didn't she wash and iron our clothes anymore? I was tired of wearing wrinkled shirts to school. Just the other day, Casey Parks had made fun of the way I was dressing now. I'd be forced to settle that score on the playground. I guess more than anything, I wondered why Mama didn't love us anymore. I was tired of her not talking to us or listening to us. Why didn't she act like Mama? Why,

why, why? My world was full of confusion and unanswered questions. I hated the word *why*.

Oh, the questions and confusion that clouded my mind. The never-ending questions and uncertainties with no explanations became consuming, massive, and terrifying. It was so hard to live in an adult world with all of its complications, heartaches, and—what did Reverend Small call them? Trials and tribulations. Yes, trials and tribulations stacked up in huge piles that seemed insurmountable at the time. No one understood my confusion and anger; no one cared to answer the smallest question. My childish vocabulary consisted of endless questions of why, why not, and when. The innocence and curiosity of childhood are meant to be blessings, but when layers of questions multiply and remain unanswered, then life becomes a frustrating experience that engrains itself forever in your heart, mind, and soul. To me, it seemed like Daddy wasn't the only one who had died.

Of course, being the tender age of ten at the time, I couldn't appreciate nor comprehend Mama's mental state or the dilemma in which she found herself. Depression or post-partum depression were not topics of everyday conversation and were not talked about outside the realms of a doctor's office. I couldn't comprehend grief's full impacts and its associating emotions. I was helplessly ignorant to the dismay my mother must have faced at this point in her young life. I couldn't rationalize these facts: she was young, thirty-four, the mother of seven kids ranging in ages from 6 months to fifteen years. As an experienced mother, she knew that kids were always hungry and needed attention. She'd never held an outside job and didn't have a high-school education, just finishing the eighth grade. Just this year, she had given birth in April, watched a beloved husband get sicker and die a horrible, slow death, and somehow had managed to keep the kids fed and the house going during July and August when Daddy was in the sanitarium. She had washed the bloody stained sheets, the once-white pillowcases, the work shirts, the worn handkerchiefs, the red-soaked towels and washcloths. It was Mama who had been strong for all of us, my father included. In the end, she had buried her husband of eighteen years. Now, when life's toils robbed her energy, sapped her strength, and diminished her resilience, she needed help, but no one realized how much—especially me. As a child, grieving for my father, grieving for my mother, and grieving for the life I once knew, I could only live in the present, which was becoming harder to do.

On this particular morning, Mary had asked me to take the garbage out to the charred barrel in the backyard where we burned our trash. Loathing this responsibility, I hurried so I could get to the bus stop in time to get Mrs. Johnson's daily supply of cookies. For some reason, maybe hunger, that's all I could think about as I trotted up the road with my spelling and arithmetic books trapped under my right arm and my pencil box rattling loudly, clutched tightly in my left hand. As I approached, I watched a scene unfold before my eyes that caused my bad mood to switch quickly to rage. My throat constricted, my temples began to pound, and my heartbeat quickened. I couldn't breathe.

Russell Thomas stood over Richard who was lying on the ground with a bloody nose and seemed stunned.

"What's goin' on here? Stop it! Lee? Hey! What's goin' on?" I angrily yelled. "What have you done to Richard? Lee, why did you let him do that to Richard?" I grabbed Lee by the wrinkled collar of his red and green plaid shirt.

Lee jerked away from me. "I didn't do it. Take it out on Russell."

Nobody was going to push my brothers and sisters around. Not even Russell Thomas and the five neighborhood cronies he called "his gang." I slowly made a 360 degree turn, defiantly staring in the faces of Russell, Terrance, Jerry, Paul, Jeff, and Todd. Then I turned to Lee. I was livid. There he stood off to the side with his hands thrust deep into his pant's pockets. He returned a sheepish look before staring down at the toes of his shoes.

"What happened, Lee?" My voice startled him. Lee shrugged in reply, not lifting his downcast eyes.

Quickly, Mary dropped to her knees in the dirt beside Richard and wiped his nose with a crumpled tissue. "Richard's okay, Roy. Richard's going to be just fine, aren't you, Richard?" She shot Russell a hateful look.

"Why don't you ask me, Roy?" asked a sneering Russell. "Are you afraid to ask me?"

"No, I'm not afraid to ask you. What happened to my brother?" I demanded.

"So peep-squeak wants to know what happened to his brother?" His loyal cronies started giggling, and Todd slapped him playfully on his back.

Russell Thomas was twelve years old and outweighed me by ten or fifteen pounds. But today, that didn't matter. I rushed at Russell who stopped laughing. I wanted to wipe that sneering smile off his ugly, freckled, snotty-nosed face. I wanted to yank his red hair out by the handfuls.

From out of no where, I remembered Daddy's voice saying, "I don't expect you to start fights, but if someone else does and there's no way around it, then you better get in the first punch. I expect you to take up for yourself and not to let people run over you. And if you don't, then you and I will have a talk. Sometimes, you just can't turn the other cheek like the good book says." Daddy was right. This was one of those times when that wasn't going to work. Richard's face was proof of that.

"Daddy, if you're looking down from Heaven, then you're about to see your advice in action right before your angelic eyes," I thought. I lowered my head, and with all my strength, I rammed Russell's stomach. He doubled over. I'd knocked the wind completely out of his body! He dropped to the gray dirt on his knees and rocked silently back and forth on the ground. Then, he began gasping for breath. While my heart pounded in my chest, my eyes were popping out of their sockets. By the way the top of my head was hurting, I just knew it was badly bruised or dented in for life. I waited to see what he'd do next, because he'd have to save face in front of his cronies. That meant I'd probably end up losing mine.

"Git up, Russell. Come on and git up! Teach him a lesson. Smash his face in! Git up! C'mon, git up!" Jeff yelled at the top of his lungs.

Russell lunged forward, and with one hard swipe of his freckled arm, my legs flew out from under me. I was lying flat on my back in the dirt. Quickly, Russell straddled me and was pounded my face on both sides. I couldn't breathe with him sitting on my chest. After his first few hits, my face mercifully became numb. My own knuckles bled as I pounded his ugly head and bony ribs. I wasn't shielding myself. At a time like this, you didn't think, you didn't feel, you didn't hear anything around you. I kept swinging blindly with all intentions of making meaningful contact. Suddenly, his pounding punches stopped as Mr. Thomas lifted Russell from my chest.

"Okay! Okay! Stop it. Stop it I said," Mr. Thomas demanded with a yell. "Stop it, Russell!" Stop swinging. Calm down."

Finally, Russell did.

"Roy, git up, son. Come on. Git up." He offered me his hand, but I declined it. Really, I just wanted to lie in the dirt and die a quick death. The numbness was leaving, and my body began aching. I trembled. "Come on, son. Git up. Give me your hand. Somebody better tell me what in the blue blazes is goin on here."

Mary and Mrs. Johnson leaned over me and began pulling my arms upwards. Even though I was still angry, I wanted to cry. But Russell Thomas would never have the satisfaction of seeing tears flowing from my two eyes. I stood on wobbly legs.

"I don't know what's up with that moron," Russell jeered looking at me. I returned a defiant stare. He pointed his index finger in my face, and I smacked it away. "See how he is? I was jest standing around, minding my own business, and he just came runnin' at me. Knocked me down on the ground." As an afterthought, he asked his gang members, "Didn't he? Didn't he just knock me down? Didn't he, Jeff?"

"Yeah, I saw the whole thing," answered Jeff. "Roy just came running up and knocked Russell down for no reason at all. I think he must be looney."

They all giggled.

"Terrance, what happened?" Mr. Thomas asked.

"Uh, well, I uh," Terrance stammered. Russell shot him a threatening stare. "Actually, if you want to know the truth, I had my back turned and didn't see anything until it had started."

"Well, why don't somebody explain why Richard's nose is bleeding," Mrs. Johnson asked softly. She turned to Richard. "Richard, why is your nose bleeding, honey?" she calmly urged.

Richard began to cry. He slowly shook his head back and forth and stared at the ground. Richard's emotions and pain had taken control. Plus, he hated conflict or violence.

"I'll tell Mr. Thomas what happened, Mrs. Johnson. I was here when everything started," Mary began. "Remember when you came to the bus stop and gave us our cookies this morning? You gave each of us a cookie, but you gave Richard two cookies. You asked Richard to give Roy a cookie because Roy wasn't here yet. He was home taking out the garbage."

"Yes, Mary. That's right. Go on." Mrs. Johnson nodded her head, urging Mary to continue.

"Well, after you left and went back into your house, Russell told Richard he wanted Roy's cookie and told him he'd better give it to him or else. But Richard wouldn't give it to him, so Russell threatened him and told him he'd hit him if he didn't. Richard still wouldn't give it to him. Richard told Russell he was keeping the cookie for Roy just like you'd asked him to do. Then out of no where, Russell just hauled off and slapped Richard across his face. That's what made Richard's nose bleed."

My pulse was raising. I felt the blood pounding in my temples.

"Russell, is that true?" Mr. Thomas demanded. "Is Mary telling the truth about what happened?"

Before Russell could answer his father, Mrs. Johnson pulled Richard to her bosom in a tight embrace. His cries were muffled. "There now, Sweetheart. You were only doing the right thing. It's just too bad this had to happen to you. Mr. Thomas, of course it's true. You can get mad at me if you want to, but I've seen Russell bully these smaller children around for years. I try to like all the children, but Russell can be a little bully at times. Russell, shame on you! It's bad enough you pick on boys your same size, but to pick on someone a lot smaller than you is wrong. If you had wanted an extra cookie, you could have asked, and I would gladly have given you one. But you didn't ask me. You need to apologize to Richard and to everyone for causing this fight this morning."

Mr. Thomas didn't know what to say, so he just watched his son. Russell's face reddened even more. "Yes, ma'am. Richard, sorry. Sorry ever'body."

"There now. That's the right thing to do, Russell. You'll feel better now," Mrs. Johnson said in her soothing, calm voice.

"Thanks Mrs. Johnson. Russell, we'll have a talk this afternoon after school," Mr. Thomas said with a threat. "Roy, are you okay?"

"Yes, sir."

Mary touched a clean tissue to her tongue and dabbed the dirt and sticky blood from my face. Then she helped me brush the dust from my clothes. She raked her fingernails through my hair like a comb, just like she did for Mama.

Lee seemed ashamed and stood off to himself. When I was calmer, I'd have a serious talk with him. In the meantime, I wasn't feeling hatred or anger towards anyone. Hatred and anger were emotionally and physically draining. Right now, I was feeling lots of pride: pride for Mary, pride for Mrs. Johnson, and especially, pride for Richard. He'd defended me in spite of Russell's threats.

Just having Richard around was like having a proven antibiotic for anything bad.

Chapter 20

Give to everyone who asks you, and if anyone takes what belongs to you, do not demand it back. Do to others as you would have them do to you.
Luke 6: 30 - 31

Richard: After the famous "cookie fight," as it was later dubbed, we climbed aboard the school bus and away from our neighborhood. Instead of sitting with Danny, who had become my best friend, I decided to sit with Roy. Russell and his gang were sitting in the back of the bus making crying noises just to further agitate Roy. We sat on a brown leather bench seat closer to the front of the bus. Mary was sitting with Lee.

"Roy?" I asked.

Roy didn't respond.

"Roy?" I asked again and nudged him with my elbow.

"Ouch! That hurts!" Roy cried while grabbing his side.

"I'm sorry. I jest wanted to give you your cookie," I said timidly. "I didn't mean for all this to happen, you know, for you to git in a fight because of me."

"Don't worry about it, Richard. Besides, you keep the cookie. You earned it. By the way, how's your nose? Hurt?"

"No, not much! I think it's stopped bleeding."

I was almost excited to have finally gotten a bloody nose. Now maybe my brothers would be proud of me. And the best part of it was, I didn't start the fight, and I didn't hit or hurt anyone.

"Yeah, it's stopped. You keep the cookie, Richard. I probably won't be hungry. I probably won't feel like eating anythin' for lunch anyhow."

I was feeling dejected, like all of this had happened for nothing. After all, if I had just gone ahead and given Russell Roy's cookie, then no one would have fought or gotten hurt. Roy seemed to read my thoughts. He always did.

"Hey, Richard. Thanks for what you did back there. You know, sticking up for me and not giving in to Russell. That took a lot of guts. I'm really proud of you!" Roy was actually smiling.

"You are?" I was amazed and a little embarrassed.

"Sure. After all, you defended my cookie."

We both laughed.

"No kidding. That was a really brave thing you did. I'll never forget it. Like I said, I'm proud of you. Daddy would have been, too."

I turned to look at my brother. "Really, Roy? Do you really think he'd been proud?"

Roy wrinkled his forehead as if he were trying to formulate the right words to say. "Hey, I don't think. I know so. Here, hand me that cookie. I think I'm getting my appetite back."

My hand dug inside my sack to locate a single-wrapped cookie. As I was reaching for the cookie, Roy ruffled my hair just like Daddy used to do. When I giggled, he looked shy.

After he finished eating every crumb of the homemade oatmeal and raisin cookie, he leaned back against the brown leather seat, folded his arms across his chest, and beamed all the way to school.

Chapter 21

If you find it in your heart to care for somebody else, you will have succeeded.
Maya Angelou

Roy: On the morning of the famous "cookie fight," as it was named by Russell and his band of pirates (anyone who'd steal a cookie from a little boy was a pirate in my book), I had the bad luck of running into the object of my affections, Miss Greene. I'd planned to go into the boys' bathroom to check my appearance. Even though I thought I looked rough, Mary had assured me I was fine.

Miss Greene stared at me as I made my way down the hall towards her. She placed a gentle hand on my shoulder, prohibiting me from entering the classroom.

"Roy, may I speak with you for just a minute?" she asked rather timidly.

"Yes, ma'am," I answered with a forced smile. Any other time, I would have enjoyed talking to her. But today was not the day. Besides, it hurt to talk. I think one of my front teeth was loose.

"Roy, you look like you were fighting this morning? Were you?"

"Yes, ma'am." I felt tiny.

"Could you tell me why?" She probed.

"I'd rather not."

"And why not?" She continued probing.

"I'm tired of thinking about it. That's all."

"I'd like an explanation if you were fighting. Please start from the beginning."

Wow. She was persistent. Finally, someone was actually interested in me for a change and that someone happened to be Miss Greene. So I didn't hold back. I spilled my guts. I embellished how I had pounded Russell Thomas' skull. I made sure she knew he was a lot older and weighed a lot more than me. I went on to tell her how I had had to beat off his other five friends—this was just a small white lie – I had to do this to defend my brother. After I finished my story, she shook her beautiful head from side to side and hugged me.

"Roy, you know fighting is wrong, but I can certainly understand why you felt the need to take up for your younger brother. It must be really hard with your father's recent death and all." She paused, gently lifted my chin, and peered straight into my brown eyes. Another jolt of electricity raced through my body. If she kept this up, I'd be electrocuted.

"Roy, I've been noticing how your hair isn't always combed. You probably haven't had a hair cut in a few weeks, either, have you? And your clothes are wrinkled and unkempt. That is so unlike you. I don't want to hurt your feelings; I just want to find out if there is something I can do to help. You have to understand. Mary was a student of mine, so I have some background knowledge of your family. Is everything okay at home? Is your mother doing okay?"

Suddenly, I wanted to crawl into the biggest crack I could find in the wooden floor beneath my feet. I felt ashamed of my hair and my wrinkled clothes. What had she called them? Unkempt? I felt dirty, smelly. I felt ashamed. Words escaped me. My throat was dry.

"I guess everythin's fine. Mama stays in bed a lot. She cries' a whole lot. Sometimes she doesn't even know when we're at home. But we're taking care of ourselves. We're managing jest fine. Mary does a lot for Lizzie and Tommy, our baby sister and brother. The rest of us do the other chores. You know, like taking the garbage out or washing the dishes."

"Well, I don't want to pry or make you feel uneasy. Will you let me know if there is anything I can do, Roy? I'll be happy to help out in any way. If you just ever need to talk, you'll let me know, won't you, Roy?" Even though her voice was sweet and she sounded like a mockingbird, all I felt was shame.

"Yes, ma'am." I needed to escape her intent stare. "Can

I go in now?"

"Sure you can." A smile parted her perfectly shaped mouth. "Go ahead."

That night before getting my bath, I asked Mary to trim my hair. Then I began another nightly routine – the one of ironing my school shirts and pants.

Chapter 22

*Trust in him at all times. O people; pour out your hearts to him, for
God is our refuge.*
Psalm 62: 8

Richard: The dreams began shortly after Thanksgiving that year. Some people say dreams are nothing to be scared of, but I knew differently. You see—most of my dreams had a tendency to come true. I don't know when I first realized it. Maybe it was when I was five and dreamed Roy broke his ankle roller-skating. I remember waking up and crying about that. Sure enough, two weeks later, he did. Then there was the dream I'd had about Daddy before we knew he was sick.

In the dream, he was standing beside a man he called his father. I had never met my grandfather because he, too, died of tuberculosis the year before I was born. Daddy was holding a little girl in his arms and laughing. He called her Neely. Whenever Daddy started to speak, blood poured out of his mouth. His father placed a padlock through Daddy's upper and bottom lips. When he inserted a golden key and turned it, the blood stopped.

Shortly after the dream, we began to realize how sick Daddy was. As long as I could remember, he'd always had a cough. Gradually, the coughing had become more persistent. Next, he started coughing up blood. For the longest time, I felt guilty about having the dream and blamed myself for him dying. One Sunday while everyone was in Sunday School, I went to Reverend Small's office where I shared some of my dreams with him. He reassured me that my dreams didn't cause anything to happen. He told me that some people have dreams that often come true, more so than other peoples' dreams. He told me about it being a God-given gift and agreed I might have it. He also told me about Neely. Neely had been our sister who was born after Mary and before Roy. Neely had died of meningitis when she was less than two years old. I didn't remember ever seeing a picture of Neely in our home. But I knew what she looked like from my dream. My grandfather, too.

That year, we ate Thanksgiving dinner at Grandma's house. Mary and Roy had stayed up late the night before washing and ironing all of our Sunday clothes. Mark said we had to make this a happy holiday even though Daddy was gone. In my heart, I knew Daddy was with us because I felt his presence all the time. On Thanksgiving morning, we all dressed in our freshly ironed clothes. Even Mama! She looked so pretty. Now when I think of Mama, that's the way I like to remember her. For several months, Mama had stayed in bed a lot and sometimes never dressed. She just slept or moped around most of the time like she was lost. Somehow the word had gotten out, because Grandma, Aunt Eliza, Uncle Russ, and Uncle Ralph started visiting us more often. Mrs. Johnson came by more frequently, too. Whenever anyone came, no matter who it was, they brought us home-cooked food and bags of groceries. We were glad because Mama wasn't up to shopping yet.

Uncle Thomas and Aunt Susan, who lived in a small town forty miles away, came by to pick us up in their brand new Buick. I imagined Daddy hopping into Uncle Thomas' shiny black car with the rest of us, riding to Grandma's house. When we arrived, Grandma's house was full of aunts, uncles, and cousins. Everyone complimented Mama on her navy blue dress, red sweater, and red heels. I thought she was radiant that day with her red lipstick and her washed and styled black hair. She acted like Mama again, so that made the holiday even better.

"Mama, you look so pretty," I told her over and over again that day. I planted a kiss on her cheek each time.

"Do you think so?" She asked with a smile. It had been so long since we'd seen Mama's beautiful smile.

"Yes! You're the prettiest Mama in the whole wide world!" I meant it.

She hugged me in response and released me way too soon. I wanted that hug to last forever, so I could feel loved again. I missed my mama so much. I guess we all did.

"You children look like you've lost weight," Grandma said. "Don't they look thin, Penny? Iris, aren't you feeding these children?" Grandma was always fussing over us. Just like Granny when she came to visit. "Well, you're gonna eat today. Grandma's gonna make sure you eat until you pop wide open!" She laughed, but if you knew anything at all about Grandma, you knew she meant that.

She shooed us out of the kitchen and into her crowded dining room where the wooden table was longer than normal. My uncles had added two saw horses and a big four by eight foot piece of plywood. This was covered with a white linen tablecloth. All kinds of chairs surrounded the table. My mouth watered as my eyes traveled over the mounds of food. I hadn't seen this much food since – well, since – since Daddy died. Finally, we all stood and held hands while Uncle Bob asked the blessing. Then we dug in.

I remember Roy sat between Aunt Penny and Cousin Patricia. Patricia was Roy's age, and he was her favorite cousin. A rumor at school said she even liked him for a boyfriend. Roy shot me one of his miserable "Roy" looks before he started shoveling forkfuls of food in his mouth. After that, he seemed fine. He even began laughing and talking to Patricia. Mary, Mark, Lee, and Lizzie seemed to be enjoying themselves and eating lots of food. Mama was laughing, so that made me happy. This was going to be a good day, after all.

After Thanksgiving at Grandma's, you always felt as stuffed as the turkey you'd eaten. I had my share of turkey and dressing, ham, candied yams with marshmallows, mashed potatoes with lots of butter, coleslaw, canned string beans, corn and green peas from Grandma's garden, homemade biscuits, pickled beets, and pickled peaches. For dessert, we had our choice of pumpkin pie, chocolate cake, egg custard, or pecan pie.

"Did everyone get enough to eat?" Grandma questioned. "There is too much food left over." The adults moaned and groaned at the thought of eating another bite. Afterwards, they went into the living room to have coffee, smoke cigarettes, and talk about grown-up stuff. All the kids, except Mark, went outside for an afternoon of fun and games. Mark looked grown up sitting beside Mama who was feeding Tommy a bottle of warmed milk.

That afternoon, we played hide-n-seek, dodge ball, jump rope, and other games until it started getting dark. Mary and cousins Essie, Patricia, and Margaret were giggling as they whispered about the boys in their classes at school. I watched as Roy and Lee followed Billy and Al behind Grandma's garage in the backyard. Curious, I followed. As I approached, I heard them snickering and talking really low. When I stuck my head around the corner, Lee saw me. I gasped.

"What the heck are you doin' spying on us?" Lee asked. An unlit cigarette dangled between his lips. "Come here, Richard. You better not tell. Okay?"

Shocked, I couldn't say a word. Roy was puffing a lit cigarette, too. He inhaled deeply and then began coughing hard. It seemed like the smoke would never stop coming out of his mouth and lungs. His face turned red as his eyes watered. Was Roy crying? His tongue was hanging out of his mouth as he coughed. I thought he was going to choke to death. Billy, Al, and Lee were doubled over laughing at Roy.

"Where did ya'll git those cigarettes?" I asked because I didn't know what else to do.

"You don't need to know. So, quit snooping around. Beat it," Lee warned. "And, remember, don't tell anyone what you saw."

"And you don't need to talk to him that way," Roy warned him in between his coughs. "Richard won't tell, will ya? Besides, I'm giving him a stick of Teaberry Gum when we git home."

"No. I won't tell. I promise." I was happy to leave them

to their mischief. Besides, Uncle Ralph was starting a game of Mother May I in the front yard. As I ran to join the game, I noticed Lizzie and three year-old Sarah. They were sitting on the back porch, clutching naked baby dolls, and rocking them back and forth like little mamas. Poor dolls!

The day ended too quickly. We hadn't had that much fun in a long time. Even Mama seemed relaxed and peaceful after spending the holiday with her family. But on the way home, our fatigue caught up with us, and we were quiet. Grandma had loaded us down with bags full of leftovers and desserts.

After we got home and said goodbye to Uncle Thomas and Aunt Susan, we put on our cotton pajamas and climbed into bed. Surprisingly, Mama appeared in our doorway. It was hard to see her face in the darkness with the living room lamp glowing behind her like a halo. She came over and kissed each of us on the foreheads.

"You are such good children. I hope you had a good Thanksgiving. We do have a lot to be thankful for, don't we?" She hesitated and laughed. "Boy I ate too much. Did you all get enough to eat?"

"Yes!" We each replied.

"Good, good. I'm glad you did. Well, sweet dreams. I love you. Good night." Her words were music to my ears.

"Good-night, Mama," I called out first. "I love you, too."

"Night, Mom," said Mark. He was lying on his back beside me. Even in the dark, I could see him smiling.

"Night, Mama," Lee called from the other bed. "Love ya."

"Night," Roy replied.

I turned my head to look at Roy. Surely, that wasn't all he was going to say. He was turned on his side with his back to the doorway. And that was all he did say.

Mama paused for a minute, then she closed the door softly. I heard giggles and the low hum of voices coming from

Mary's bedroom. Lizzie and Tommy were asleep, Lizzie in Mama's bed, and Tommy in his crib in her room. When she walked outside on the front porch, I was still awake. I heard the squeaky porch swing moving back and forth. I wondered what she was thinking about? Was she missing Daddy? Had Roy hurt her feelings. Too tired to think, the swing's squeaking sounds lulled me into a deep sleep. That's when I had the dream about Mark.

"Mark! Mark!" I called. "Why are you dressed in that suit?"

"It's a uniform, little brother. I'm going away for a little while, but you'll be okay. How do you like my white uniform?" He was beaming from pride and standing tall. Mark was handsome and appeared to be grown-up.

I began to cry. "You can't go away, Mark. I'll miss you. You have to stay with us. We need you. Mama needs you. Please take off the uniform and stay with us. Promise me you won't go away." I was begging.

"I have to go away, Richard," he said gently. Mark sat beside me and ruffled my hair. "I am doing this for all of us. It's the best thing. You have to understand. It's the best thing for all of us. Hey, look! They're coming to get me now!" He pointed to something in the fog that surrounded us.

I was scared. "Whose coming to get you, Mark? Where are you going? Are you going to Heaven to be with Daddy? Is that where you're going? I'll ask Jesus if you can stay. He won't make you go. Don't go, Mark. Don't leave us. We need you."

He reached out his hand and started backing away. He was smiling as he placed a small cap on his head. His shoes were the shiniest black shoes I'd ever seen.

"Besides, you have the key. God takes care of those who have the key. Help the others, Richard. Help them find the key. They need your help. Pop will take care of you while I'm gone, so don't worry. Everything will be okay."

"What key? Mark! What key?"

None of what Mark was saying made any sense to me. I couldn't see him. He'd disappeared into a dense, dark fog. I began crying.

"Mark! Mark! Where are you? Please come back. I can't see you anymore." I ran after him, but the fog was even thicker. I was scared. "Where are you? Please come back. What key? Who is Pop? Tell me before you go," I pleaded. But it was no use. He was gone, and I was sobbing uncontrollably.

I heard Mark's faint voice in the distance like an echo in a cave. I couldn't see him, but I heard his far-away voice getting closer.

"Richard! Richard! Wake up. You're dreaming." Mark was shaking me hard. "Richard, wake up. Stop crying."

I was relieved to find I was in our bed lying beside Mark. Mark was here!

"I'm awake," I finally said. I turned my wet pillow over.

"Yeah, so are we," groaned Lee.

"Shut up. He can't help it," Roy said. "Richard. What's wrong? What were you dreaming about?"

"Nothin's wrong. I'm okay. I just had a nightmare. Sorry." Actually, I was really embarrassed.

"That's okay," Roy whispered. "Having to sleep in the same room with Lee would make anyone have nightmares!"

"Oh, cut it out," Lee groaned. "Look whose talking."

They started smacking each other playfully.

"Hey, guys. Let's get back to sleep," Mark suggested.

"All right. Night!" Roy said.

"Night everybody," Lee echoed.

"Night," I said while looking around the dark room to reassure myself. No fog. No white uniform. Mark perched on his elbow beside me. His dark hair was rumpled, and he wore a worried frown. He peered down at me in the darkness and whispered, "Hey, little buddy, are you okay?"

"Yeah, I'm fine." Then I began to cry.

"Tell me what it is."

"Mark. I'm so glad you're here. I dreamed you were leavin' us and going away. You were wearin' a white uniform. You were in a thick fog, and I couldn't find you. And you kept talking about a key. Some key that I had. Oh, and you were talking about Pop taking care of us. It was scary. Mark, promise you aren't goin' anywhere. Promise you won't leave."

Mark was silent for a long time. Finally, he whispered, "I'm here, ain't I?" Then he tickled my armpits until I started giggling. "Now, go back to sleep. No more dreams, promise?"

"Okay. I promise."

I closed my eyes and tried to drift off to sleep, but I couldn't. Something was bothering me. After a while, I heard Mark's soft, nasal snores. As I listened to his rhythmic sounds, I suddenly realized what was bothering me. Mark had never promised!

Chapter 23

At the side of the everlasting why, is a yes, and a yes, and a yes.
E.M. Forster

Roy: The next day was another happy day. We were out of school for Thanksgiving holiday when Granny came for an unannounced visit. We were outside playing racehorses when we saw her waddling down the street towards our house. She had taken the train from Charlotte early that morning. The city bus had dropped her off at the end of the street. We hadn't seen Granny since Daddy died in September. But she had telephoned us frequently to stay in touch with how we were doing.

At the time, I didn't know it, but Mary had kept Granny informed about Mama's demeanor during the weeks following Daddy's death. While it was true that Mama hadn't been herself for a while, things were getting better. Starting yesterday, she was dressing each morning, quite different from the days of bathrobes and nightgowns. For the past two days, she'd cooked our breakfast and was taking care of Tommy. Today, she'd even helped Mary and me clean the house. Mary and I had taken over the washing and the ironing. I was insistent on ironing my own clothes each night before bedtime.

After Granny waddled up the five steps leading to the porch, she stopped to wipe tiny beads of sweat from her forehead with a man's linen handkerchief she pulled from her bosom. After catching her breath, she started laughing and hugged Richard, Lee, and me really hard. She plastered kisses on our dirty foreheads and said in that Scot-Irish brogue we loved so dearly, "Well, top of the day to ya, little ones. How are ya?"

"Granny! Granny!" Mary heard her voice and came running out of the house to embrace her. "I'm so glad you're here!"

"Me, too. Me, too." She laughed and hugged Mary.

"What a pretty lassie you are. You truly are a red rose and a sight for old eyes. Now, can an ol' lady get a drink o' water around here?" she asked as she fanned herself with the damp handkerchief.

Mary led her into the house with us following close behind. Mama heard our commotion and abruptly stopped in the kitchen's doorway when she saw Granny. She wiped tiny remnants of fresh dough from her hands onto her apron and half-smiled. "Why Mother Anna. What are you doing here? I didn't know you were coming for a visit. Isn't this a surprise?"

I noticed she didn't say "nice" surprise. Did I detect confusion and, perhaps, a little anger beneath her smile? This wasn't the way she used to act when Granny came to visit.

"Hello, Iris. I hope it is okay. I just wanted to visit with me grandchildren. I wanted to make sure ya were okay. Besides, I thought ya might could use some help."

"Well, of course it's okay! You know you're always welcome here. We've actually been fine. Just fine, haven't we children?" Before we could answer, she continued. "Come in the kitchen, and let me get you a glass of tea."

"Water's fine." Grandma turned and winked at us.

"Okay. Well, come into the kitchen and sit down. You must be tired. Tell us all about your trip while I fix supper."

Mary didn't seem to notice Mama's strange reaction to Granny's unannounced arrival. Granny related the events of her morning train ride from Charlotte and how the conductor was afraid she couldn't get through the middle aisle. She had us laughing, even Mama. When she finished the glass of water, Mary refilled it. Granny stopped talking so she could pat Mary's hand.

"Thanks, Mary. Yes, Iris. Just the other day, I began feeling guilty about not being here to help ya out with the children and the house. There's no reason for me to sit around that big old house when I can be here with all of you. Besides, I made my Randall, God bless his soul, a promise that I'd help watch over ya, and that's exactly what I aim to do."

Now that Granny was here, maybe everything would be normal again. Well, as normal as it could be. Did I hear Mama groan when she left the kitchen to check on Tommy?

"Okay, children. Tell me about school and your friends." Granny had a way of making us feel important and loved. Somehow the simple things of our lives seemed like giant things to her.

When Mark got home, he seemed extremely pleased to see Granny. Granny just cheered up a place with her presence. Mark wrapped his skinny arms around her and hugged hard.

"Mark, don't break me! Ya look like you're losing weight! Are ya working too hard, boy? Is that it? And besides, what's this I hear about ya not going to school? Do ya think your daddy would be pleased with that decision? He felt strongly about ya children getting an education. I can't believe ya quit high school before ya even started it."

"Well, Granny, I did intend to go to school, but I felt like we really needed the money. I felt like this was the best decision for all of us. I'm selling newspapers in the morning, and then I help Uncle Russ in the afternoon." Mark lowered his eyes from her penetrating stare. No one said anything for a while until Granny broke the silence.

"What did ya say? Money? Ya need money?" She seemed confused and displeased with his response. And it took a lot to anger Granny - even with her Scot-Irish temperament.

Mama was staring at Mark in a disapproving way.

"Well, you're a good boy, Mark o' me heart. And your daddy would be proud o' ya, too, and the way you care about your family. This is a big sacrifice on your part. Besides, it's none o' me business if your mama is okay with it."

Mark seemed relieved.

Mama interrupted and barked orders. "Supper is almost ready. Mary, will you help me set the table? Roy, how about you and Lee getting the tea glasses ready? Richard, check on Tommy, and make sure he's still asleep. Mark, just go ahead and get washed up. And Lizzie, get that thumb out of your mouth. You're going to have bucked baby teeth if you don't stop."

Mama didn't talk too much during supper, so Granny tried to take up the slack by telling funny stories to make us laugh. After supper, Granny asked us if we'd had a nice Thanksgiving.

"Yes, we did," Mary replied. "We ate with Grandma. All the aunts and uncles and cousins were there. It was fun! And Grandma cooks so good, just like you do. I love to eat at Grandma's house. It's the first time we've had that much food in a long time."

Mama didn't seem pleased with Mary's last comment and acted bored with the conversation.

"Roy, it's your turn to help me wash dishes," Mama said.

"Again? Why doesn't Mark ever have to help wash the dishes?" I asked.

"Roy!" she scolded. "Mark works all day long. Besides, don't ever question me again."

"Yes, ma'am." I was embarrassed being scolded in front of Granny, but I guess I deserved it.

"Lee, you can help Roy by drying and putting away the dishes. Mary, will you help Lizzie with her bath while I give Tommy his supper?"

"Yes, ma'am." Mary left the room tugging Lizzie's arm.

Granny touched the Bible on the coffee table. I saw Richard reach over to pick it up.

"I love the book of Ruth. It's about love in its purest form. Can you read it to me, Richard?"

He turned through the Bible until he found the book of Ruth. As we washed supper dishes, we heard Richard reading and stumbling through the words. Granny, who seemed genuinely pleased with his progress, interjected compliments from time to time. Somehow, I felt reassured that Granny was here. And the best part was she hadn't said when she planned to leave.

Chapter 24

Don't let anyone look down on you because you are young, but set an example for the believers in speech, in life, in love, in faith and in purity. Until I come, devote yourself to the public reading of Scripture, to preaching and to teaching. Do not neglect your gift.
I Timothy 4: 12 - 14

Richard: During the weeks leading up to Christmas, Granny arose each morning to cook our breakfast. Then she'd take care of Lizzie and Tommy so Mama could resume her daily house chores, including the washing and ironing, except for Roy's clothes. He insisted on ironing his own pants and shirts every night before bed. Mama even began grocery shopping again. She went through each day hardly ever smiling, not even when we'd rush home from school with a special drawing we'd made for her or to surprise her with a good grade. Mama wasn't happy, and it was obvious.

Granny tried to smooth things over by complimenting us and making us feel good about our drawings and grades. As hard as she tried to be a substitute for Mama, she just wasn't Mama. The last time I remembered Mama telling me that she loved me was when she told all of us on Thanksgiving night. She seemed mad about something. I couldn't think of anything we'd done. Maybe she was mad because Granny was here. That's when I began praying every night for Jesus to make Mama happy again. I prayed that if Daddy was hovering around, he'd find a way to make her laugh like he used to.

After school one day, Granny asked me to go outside with her to the porch. It was unseasonably warm, so I sat on the plank floor while she rocked back and forth in the squeaky porch swing. She seemed really quiet.

"Granny, do you want me to read you the Bible?" I asked.

"No, Richard. I wanted to talk to ya. Just ya." She lowered the wire-framed glasses on her broad nose and peered over the rims. "Richard, let me tell ya something about me. It's special and not too many people will even care or understand. I don't tell a lot of people about it."

"Is it a secret?" I asked.

"Yeah, well, sort of, I guess. Here's the secret. I was born with a veil over me face. Sometimes, it's called a caudle. Do ya know what that means?"

"No, Granny. I don't understand a 'veil'. Are ya talking about what women wear to church each Sunday?" She had my undivided attention.

"No, not that kind of veil. It's just a covering over your face, but not like a lady's veil."

"Well, then, what is it?"

"Well, let me explain it this way. God gives all of us talents and gifts. He gives us these things to help other people. Some people have the talent to teach others, while some people have the talent to serve others in different ways. Some people are good at encouraging people when they're feelin' low. Some people are good at leading and others are good at following. And then some people have what's called the gift of prophecy."

"What is that, Granny? What is prophecy?"

"It's sort of like predicting the future or somehow knowing ahead of time what might happen before it actually does. It's seeing things that others don't see. That's prophecy. Ya remember some of the prophets from the Bible, don't ya? Prophets like Isaiah, Jeremiah, and Elijah?"

"Uh-huh. I think so," I replied, nodding my head.

"Well, ya have this gift, too, Richard. Just like me, ya were born with a veil over your face. When that happens, people say it's a sign that God has given ya the gift of prophecy. I don't think ya have to have a veil to have it, but people say it's a sign if you do." She paused for my thoughts to catch up.

"Where is it? I've never seen the veil before. Did Mama

keep it? Can I see it?"

"No. It's not something ya keep, Richard. When you're born, the midwife or the doctor takes it away. But the important thing for ya to remember is that God has given ya a special gift. As you grow older, you'll begin to understand it more. Can ya understand anything I'm telling ya?"

"A little, I guess."

"Okay. Then let me ask ya this. Do ya ever know something before it will happen?" she queried.

"Sort of. Sometimes I dream dreams that are scary. Some dreams even come true. Sometimes, not all the time." It felt good to finally talk to someone about this.

She took a deep breath and stared at the magnolia tree in the front yard.

"Have ya been having any dreams since your father died?"

"Yes ma'am. I dream almost every night. I used to dream a lot before he died, too."

"Are there any special dreams that you remember?"

She sat quietly and listened while I told her about my dream when Roy broke his ankle. Next, I told her about the dream where Daddy was holding Neely. I told her of others. Then I told her the dream about Mark.

"I've been dreaming a lot about Mark. In all my dreams, he's got this white suit on. He's in a dark fog and he says he's going away. I always wake up cryin'."

She looked off into the distance. Do you have other dreams?"

"Well, the other one is about us."

"Who is us?" She pried.

"Me and Roy and Mary and Lizzie and Lee. Tommy's not in the dream. We're playing games in this big yard. There are lots of buildings around us. Lots of kids watching us play. And there's a church in the middle of the yard. Whenever I see the church, I feel happy, like everything's all right. Even when I wake up, I'm not afraid. I only cry when I have the

Mark dream."

Granny stopped swinging. "Would it surprise ya if I was having the same dreams you've been havin?"

"Wow! You have?"

"Yes. I have been."

"That's scary, Granny. Don't you think it's scary?"

"No, not really. It goes back to what I told ya earlier. We have a special gift, Richard. It's nothing to be afraid of. It's something to be thankful for."

"Do you think the Mark dream might come true?"

"I don't know, Richard, but it's probably really possible. If it does come true, I don't think it's bad. I don't think you have anything to worry about."

"Sometimes I can't help it. I do worry, 'cause I don't want anybody else to go away."

"I know. I understand. As Christians, we know that the things that hurt us help us to grow into better people. No matter what happens, we have to remember to put our faith in God because he will take care of us. He promises us that."

"Like Daddy dyin' and all? That hurt. Will it make me better?"

"Yes, like your daddy dyin'. That hurts bad, but we have to believe that he's happier where he is. We believe that God knows what was best for him and for all of us, don't we?"

"Yes."

"We should always pray for God's will to be done in our lives. Even though God's will isn't what we always understand, we have to have faith." Then she paused and leaned forward. "Richard, let's keep our gift and our dreams to ourselves for now, okay?"

"Sure. It's a secret! I like having secrets with you." I felt special.

"Yeah, it's a secret," she agreed. "Come here."

When I climbed to my feet, she wrapped short, flabby arms around me. "I love ya, Richard. I love all my grandchildren very much. Remember this - Granny is always with ya, no matter what happens. Can ya remember that?"

"Yes ma'am." I remembered Daddy had promised the same thing.

Lee ran through the yard. "Hey, Richard, wanna play ball? We're getting' up a game of touch football," offered Lee. "Wanna be our center?"

Granny motioned for me to go. I tried unsuccessfully to wink at her, but I ended up blinking both eyes. She laughed.

"Whose the quarterback?" I shouted while running down the steps.

"Pop's the quarterback."

I stopped running and just stood there thinking. Pop? Who was Pop? Where had I heard that name before? I couldn't remember.

"Whose Pop?" I yelled to my brother's back. He was disappearing down the street and turning into the vacant lot beside Mrs. Johnson's house.

"Lee, who is Pop?" I yelled again.

Then I heard Lee's simple reply. "Roy! It's his new nick-name."

"Why?" I questioned.

"His hero is Pop Warner, the greatest football coach who ever lived."

Chapter 25

I think that if you shake the tree, you ought to be around when the fruit falls to pick it up.
Mary Cassatt

Roy: It is amazing how one man's simple possessions can become the treasures of others. We go through our entire lives saying "I want this," "I just have to have that." We buy the necessities, we purchase favorite objects to call our own, we collect, we own, we hoard, we possess. But in the end, we leave the world as we entered it—unadorned, unblemished, naked of all possessions.

Whenever I think about Granny's visit after Thanksgiving, I remember how hard she tried to re-create some normalcy in our lives. It took a few days of nagging before Granny could convince Mama to get rid of Daddy's clothes. Many of his shirts and pants were splattered with wood varnish or dried blood. Actually, it was hard to tell the difference between the two stains.

"Roy, here, son. Take these clothes outside to the barrel and burn them. No one can use these. They're so stained." Granny was steadily pulling the clothes off wire hangers, while Mama pouted. "His dress clothes can be given away. They're too large for Mark or any of you. We'll give them to the Salvation Army. I think I'll wash them in scalding water and strong detergent, first though. Mary, start some pots of water boiling, and we'll soak the clothes in your mama's washing machine."

We just stood there like little soldiers, waiting for our next orders. Even though Mama wasn't saying anything, her face said everything. She wasn't happy, but it really didn't matter. General Granny was in charge of this mission.

"Well, what are ya standing there for? We've got lots of work to do," Granny ordered. She wedged her large frame farther into the closet to grab more clothes. I held my breath because we'd be in big trouble if she got stuck and couldn't back out.

Lee and I stuffed Daddy's clothes into the rusty, bottomless trash barrel. Lee enjoyed striking matches and stoking the fire with an iron stake.

"Here, lemme do that," I demanded.

"Naw. I had the matches first," Lee replied.

"Granny told me to do this. Not you," I countered.

"It don't matter. I'm the one with the matches."

"Kiss my foot."

"Kiss mine."

Mama was standing at the back screened door. "You boys quit that. You have better things to do than fight all the time," Mama yelled. "Lee, run and ask Mrs. Johnson if she has any headache powders. Tell her I'll pay her back sometime this week when I go to the market."

"What da'ya need headache powders for, Mama?" Lee asked.

Lee had a question for everything. Headache powders were used for headaches, right? Not for stomachaches, not for backaches, not for other aches—for headaches, right? What a moron!

"Are you stupid?" I asked in a low tone so Mama couldn't hear.

"Naw. Are you?"

"Lee, run along." Mama turned and disappeared into the house.

I struck a match and pressed it to one pant leg. In a matter of minutes, all the clothes were burning. I sat alone on the chilly grass and watched the smoke and escaping ashes drift sideways before rising and finally disappearing somewhere close to Heaven.

We spent that Saturday morning soaking the salvageable clothes in the wringer-washer Daddy had surprised Mama with earlier in the year. After the water cooled, Mary and Granny took turns feeding clothes to the two hungry rollers. I always liked to watch this process: dripping wet clothes on one side of the rollers and flattened, damp clothes on the other side.

Afterwards, Lee and I hung each piece on the wire clothesline with wooden clothespins. Clothespins had always fascinated me. They were simply two pieces of wood joined together by a spring, but they worked. I hid one in my pants pocket. I'd use it tonight on Lee's nose. His nostrils were getting a little too wide, and his snoring was driving me crazy.

A pair of khaki-colored pants flapping in the soft breeze caught my attention. It seemed weird having Daddy's things all strung out for the world to see. A lump in my throat got bigger, and my eyes watered. I wished the clothes were moving because of the man who wore them—not because of an autumn breeze.

After supper, Mary disappeared outside with the wicker clothes basket. When she returned, the basket was full of the dried clothes. While Lee and I played checkers on the living room floor, Mary, Mama and Granny lovingly folded each article of clothing and placed them in cardboard boxes marked, "Salvation Army." Richard was thumbing through the pages of an old picture book when he noticed the name on the boxes.

"What's the Salvation Army, Granny?" Richard asked.

"It's a wonderful organization that helps people. They will take these clothes and give them to people who can use them."

"Do we have to give them all away?" he asked.

"Sure, why not? Don't you want to help needy people?" She asked as she continued folding a shirt.

"Can't we keep any of them?" he persisted.

Granny stopped folding the blue shirt and hugged it to her bosom. "I don't think we should. I think Randall would've wanted his clothes given to people who could use them. These clothes will mean a lot to someone who is down on his luck." She stopped talking and paused for a minute.

"Why? Are you afraid you won't have anything left of your daddy's? Is that what's bothering ya?" she asked him.

"Yes, ma'am," Richard responded quickly. "I don't mean to be selfish, but I miss Daddy. I want something to remember him by."

"Sure ya do, and it's only normal for ya to want something of his. I'm sorry. I haven't been thinking, have I?"

We stopped playing checkers to listen to their conversation.

"Ya know what? I miss him, too. He was me second child, me first boy. I'll never forget the day he was born. I laid him on his stomach, but no. He wasn't goin' to have that. He straightened his little arms and lifted himself up. Then he held his wee little head up. People don't believe me, but it's true. I knew then that I had a strong-willed son. And he was. Your grandpa was so excited to have a boy! I think that was one of his happiest moments. He went out and bought Randall a puppy. I laughed at his silliness. What would a wee baby do with a puppy? It just made another mess for me to clean up!" She had us all laughing. "But they grew up together. I think that dog lived to be 14 or 15." Then she grew serious. "You know. Tis a hard thing for a mama to outlive her child. Tis the hardest thing I've had to live through. Nary day goes by that I don't miss my Randall. But it is my faith that keeps me going. I know that one day I'll see my boy again in Heaven."

"How do you know that, Granny?" Lee asked.

"Because we're promised that whosoever believes in Jesus and asks for forgiveness of his sins will go to Heaven. I know Randall believed and I believe. That's what gets me through each day. Knowing that makes me happy." She touched an index finger to her right temple, then to the left side of her chest. She spread her five fingers and let her hand spread over her heart.

"He left me with wonderful memories that I'll never forget." She paused. "No one can ever take those memories away. They're priceless. And he left me with a heart full o'love that I can share with all of ya'. Those are things ya just can't wash and put in a cardboard box. Ya know what else? He gave each of ya priceless treasures, too. See? Put ya hands o'er ya hearts."

We silently obeyed the gray-haired lady.

"Do ya feel ya hearts beating?" she asked.

Our heads bobbed up and down.

"That's the priceless treasure he helped give ya. He gave ya life and a big heart to love others. Think about it. He loved ya, didn't he? And ya loved him, didn't ya? Loving is what makes us human. We all want to love and to be loved. And Jesus was our best example of that. God loved us so much, he gave us his only son so that we can live forever. For me, that's the key to life. And even though your daddy's not here, ya haven't stopped loving him, have ya? Of course not! Love goes on forever. It never stops; it never dies. Your daddy's love for ya will go on forever. He's always with ya, too, because he's a part of each one of ya. Isn't that a wonderful thing to always remember? Wherever ya go, whatever ya do, your daddy is with you. So your daddy gave ya a part of himself, and that's the most priceless treasure anyone can ever give."

We were speechless as a feeling of peace permeated the room. We sat silently trying to digest everything she had said. We appreciated her simple eloquent words and hungered for more. Finally, she broke the silence to feed our souls again.

"I'm sure your mama has things to give you. But always remember that it is more important to leave love and beautiful memories behind than it is to leave things. These verses come to me mind. The Bible says, 'Lay not up for yourselves treasurers upon earth, where moth and rust doth corrupt, and where thieves break through and steal; but lay up for yourselves treasurers in Heaven, where neither moth nor rust doth corrupt, and where thieves do not break through nor steal; for where your treasure is, there will your heart be also.'"

Her eyes twinkled when she smiled and stretched out her flabby arms. We ran to her and wallowed in the security of her love. One by one, she embraced us. I never wanted to leave the shelter of her arms. After a while, she shuffled back to the basket of clothes and grabbed another wrinkled shirt to fold.

"Did I ever tell ya about the time your daddy ate fifteen green apples in one sittin? Boy, what a stomachache he had!"

She shared anecdote after anecdote from our father's childhood. The stories mingled with laughter were music to our ears, and Granny had sensed we needed a new song.

Chapter 26

Dominion belongs to the Lord and he rules over the nations.
Psalm 22:28

Richard: Unfortunately, Mama and Granny began arguing a few days before Christmas. Mama's resentment for Granny's ceaseless advice became apparent. They were arguing because Granny thought Mama should give us some of Daddy's belongings. She argued that Randall would want it that way. In the end, Mama's resistance was worn down, and Granny did persuade Mama to divide Daddy's simple little trinkets among us. Mama chose to do that on Christmas Eve when she called us all together after the supper dishes were done.

We were so excited about Santa Claus coming later that night. Packages covered with brightly colored paper and pretty bows circled the cedar Christmas tree in the corner of our living room. Lots of red and white peppermint candy canes hung on the branches. We couldn't wait to dig into these gifts from Mrs. Johnson.

Granny watched our solemn-faced mother closely from her seat on the living room sofa. For some reason, Granny seemed intent and curious about Mama's actions. There were few smiles between them when we gathered in various spots on the floor around the room and waited.

"Mother Anna and I have agreed that I should go ahead and give you some of your father's things. After all, Randall would have wanted you to have them."

Granny folded her short little arms across her massive chest and nestled deeper into the sofa's plump cushions to watch.

Mama continued, "I want this Christmas to be a special time for you, so maybe it will be. You know, we're not rich people, and your daddy didn't have a lot of personal belongings, but what he had was special to him. I hope you'll remember to take care of these little things and treasure them since they belonged to your father." Mama appeared teary-eyed.

"Mark, here's your father's gold pocket watch. Since you're the oldest, it belongs to you. Actually, he planned to give it to you when you graduated, huh, graduated from high school. It belonged to his father, right, Anna?"

Granny smiled. "Yes, it did. It was my wedding gift to your grandpa when we were married. It belonged to my father before him. Papa had purchased it in Ireland before he came to this country."

"Gosh! Ireland! Wow!" Mark exclaimed. Mama transferred the precious time-piece into Mark's eager hands. Mark raised his golden treasure to his ear to hear its ticking music. I remember his sparkling eyes. "Thanks, Mama. I remember how much this watch meant to Daddy. I'll take care of it. Thanks." You couldn't wipe the smile off Mark's face.

"You're welcome." She seemed a little more relaxed. "And now that you're occasionally shaving, take his razor and shaving mug, too. Here, they're yours."

Mark nodded. "Thanks."

Granny laughed. "And, I'd suggest ya begin using it on a daily basis, young man. That peach fuzz is getting thicker and darker all the time. You want girls to like ya, don't ya?"

He blushed. "Sure. I guess so."

"Teresa Thomas already does," Lee chided.

I held my breath as Mama picked up a black leather book. "Mary, this is your daddy's Bible. It was my wedding gift to him. I can't lie to you and tell you your daddy read it very much, but I did notice there are some verses underlined. These must have been special to him."

I was happy for Mary. She deserved Daddy's Bible. Her hands were shaking when she took the Bible from Mama and hugged it to her chest. "I hoped you'd give me his Bible. Thanks, Mama." Mary sat beside Granny and curled her legs under her. She leafed through the onion-papered pages to find the underlined phrases.

"Roy. Come here. I thought of you when I found these in your daddy's drawer. Anna, the children probably don't know this about their father, but your daddy was an expert swimmer. I bet you didn't know that he'd won several swimming awards when he was in school."

"I knew. Daddy told me about them on the way to work some mornings. We used to talk a lot," Mark replied.

"Swimming awards? No one around here gives swimming awards," stated Roy.

Mama seemed more at ease, like she was starting to enjoy this. "You'll have to remember. Daddy grew up in Charlotte. Evidently, the schools there gave swimming awards. Well, anyway, when we were first married, we used to go to the beach a lot—almost every weekend during the summer. We went with all our friends. Uncle Ralph used to tag along. Well, they always ended up having a swimming contest." She was laughing now. "Whoever was the first one to reach the end of the Carolina Beach pier won. Well, your daddy always won. No one could beat him. Right, Mother Anna?"

"Right. I've never seen anything to beat it. He could swim almost as good as he could walk," laughed Granny. "Always could."

Before we could interrupt with questions, Mama continued with her story. "Here's the amazing thing. If I hadn't seen it with my own two eyes, I wouldn't have believed it. Randall could push a small sailboat out against the tide to the end of the pier, turn around, and bring it back again. He loved to go swimming. I'm glad he taught you to swim. He thought everyone needed to know how."

"I guess I'll teach Lizzie and Tommy," Mark said smiling.

"Good," Mama said. "Daddy would want that, Mark."

"Was Daddy in the Olympics?" Lee asked.

"No." She started laughing again. "No, Daddy wasn't in the Olympics, Lee."

Mama opened a tiny cardboard box and removed some cotton. When she lifted a dark blue ribbon, a circular bronze medal was attached to the end.

"Here's one of the first place medals your daddy won, Roy. There are others. I'll give them to you. This one was his favorite because it was the first one he was awarded." I watched Mama proudly squeeze the medal piece before placing it in the middle of Roy's open palm. She gently took his fingers and closed them around the medal. "You're our little competitor, so I hope this shows how you're a chip off the old block. Do you remember how Daddy could do a jackknife?" she asked him.

Roy nodded. I remembered, too. Daddy's actions seemed so graceful. He'd jump into the air, bend his body double, touch his toes, extend his body again, and enter the water with hardly a splash. "Poetry in motion," he'd laugh and say.

"Yes. Thanks, Mama. There's nothing I'd rather have," Roy said quietly.

"Lee, your turn. Your daddy was a member of the Moose Lodge. I want you to have Daddy's lapel pin. Remember all the honorary pall bearers at the funeral? They were his friends from the lodge. Your daddy was well-liked and well-respected as a business owner. If you'll remember, he always wore this pin on his suit jacket. He was proud of this pin and being a member of the Lodge. So, it's your pin now."

"Thanks, Mama!" Lee beamed from ear to ear. "Can I get a suit so I can wear it on my label, too?"

"Lapel, son. The word is lapel." Mama corrected him. "It might be a while before we can afford to buy you a suit, but we'll see."

Lee disappeared into our bedroom. We heard him rummaging in the closet. When he returned, he was wearing his wool coat with the pin fastened to his lapel. From that day on, you'd always find this pin on Lee's lapels. It became his fondest treasure.

"Richard, I have something special for you. It's your daddy's key ring. He got this last Christmas. See? It's engraved with his initials. If you want, we can take off his keys."

"No! I want to keep them all." Gently I took my treasure. "Yes. I want to keep them all." Maybe these were the keys Mark talked about in my dream.

"Sure. You can keep them. Here. Let me show you. This is his house key." She hesitated, fingering the key lovingly. "You know, this house meant a lot to your daddy since he helped build it for us. Having a home was important to him. I remember how proud he was the first day we moved in. Daddy loved us so much, he wanted us to always be together in this home." She hesitated long enough for the mist to dry in her eyes.

"Oh, and look at this!" She laughed. "This is the key to an old truck—the first truck he ever bought. I think he worked all summer long to buy that truck after he turned sixteen, didn't he, Anna?"

Granny nodded and laughed. "He surely did. Wouldn't even stop long enough to eat. Lost a lot of weight that summer. He just had to earn enough money to buy that ugly old beat-up truck. But he loved it and kept it shined up."

Mama smiled to herself. "Evidently, he kept the spare key after he sold it."

"Why did he sell it, Mama?" I asked.

"We were getting married. He wouldn't hear of me riding around in a truck, so he sold it and bought a car. Our first car."

She started to tear up, but Mama began talking again. "Richard, this one must be the key to the shed out back. I don't know what these two are – maybe the key to his shop? I don't know. Your daddy was a key collector, it seems. Anyway, I hope you'll be proud of the key ring since it has his initials engraved on it."

I kissed Mama on the cheek. "I am proud. Thanks, Mama. It's the best Christmas present ever."

Finally, Mama lifted Lizzie and put her in her lap. "Lizzie, get that thumb out of your mouth. Daddy had a favorite lace handkerchief that was mine. I gave it to him when we were courting, uh, dating. Daddy carried it with him for good luck. He kept it on the table beside his hospital bed. I'm going to save this and give it to you when you're older. Okay?"

Sleepy Lizzie didn't reply, she just snuggled her head under Mama's chin and closed her eyes. Mama looked around the room. "Happy?"

"Yes, ma'am," we shouted.

"Good! Well, it's time for bed or Santa won't come."

I looked over at Mary who was smiling at me. Then I remembered Tommy.

"Mama, what about Tommy? Does he git somethin'?" I asked.

"Yes, Richard. Tommy's going to get Daddy's wallet when he's older. It has a picture of me and some pictures of you, kids. I thought he'd enjoy having those." Mother Anna, aren't you tired? I know I am."

"Yes, I am." Granny seemed very pleased with Mama. Daddy's small trinkets were safely distributed to her grandchildren. She sighed and heaved her heavy body forward to stand. "Come on, boys. I'll tuck ya in. Mary, I'll check on ya in a wee bit."

After we climbed into bed, Granny came in and sat on the foot of the bed Lee and Roy shared. Then she recited the Irish blessing that we had grown to love and anticipate each night. Roy's eyes sparkled in the dark like tiny lights.

May the road rise up to meet ya,
May the wind be always at your back,
May the sunshine be warm upon your face,
May the rain fall soft upon your fields,
And until we meet again,
May God hold you in the hollow of his hand.

I slept with the key ring that night, and on Christmas morning, I placed the key ring and keys in my special treasure box. It was the wooden box Daddy made last summer when he buried our treasure beside the big oak tree. I'd claimed it early on to store my marbles, gum, and the infamous treasure map. I'd also taken one of Daddy's clean handkerchiefs to wrap Tommy's money, a sprig of Mama's hair, some old string I'd found, and one of Mrs. Johnson's homemade cookies for posterity.

No one would ever replace Granny in our hearts. Christmas was special that year, not because of the toys and gifts Santa Claus brought. It was special because we knew our father's love was eternal. It was because we knew memories lived forever in your mind and in your heart. The best presents that year were Daddy's things. Love made that Christmas special, and it was Granny who helped us find the way."

Chapter 27

Hope is the thing with feathers that perches in the soul and sings the tune without the words and never stops, at all.
Emily Dickinson

Roy: After the first of the new year, Mama seemed to grow sullen and depressed. We felt a little more of her slipping away from us gradually day after day. As her spirits sunk deeper, she stayed in bed longer each morning. Even when Grandma or our aunts or uncles visited, she just didn't smile or seem like herself. No longer was she pretentious or wore a "smiling" face for Granny's benefit. I can't explain how grateful and relieved I was that Granny was with us.

        Aging Granny took on more and more of the household chores and tried to tend to Lizzie and Tommy while we were in school. By the time the bus dropped us off in the afternoon, Granny was worn-out and began slowing down. We were too young to understand or realize how emotionally and physically drained she was. She sacrificed her health for us. Eventually, in order to save herself, she had to leave us. So, when her dreaded announcement came in early March, we were deeply saddened and dismayed. We tried everything from crying real tears to begging her to stay to drawing her pictures in art class. We did all our chores without reminders and ate all our food. I continued ironing my own clothes. We offered her anything to stay, but she just wouldn't – she couldn't.

        We miserably walked with her to the end of the street where she'd catch the city bus to the train station. She smothered us with kisses and bear hugs before heaving her large frame up the bus's steps. Not even the ugly red sign could stop her.

        On March 26, Mark celebrated his sixteenth birthday by nonchalantly announcing he wanted to join the Navy. We had just finished eating the chocolate birthday cake that Mrs.

Johnson had made especially for Mark. Of course, we were all stunned and deeply hurt. Mary and Richard immediately began crying, while Lee and I just stared incredulously at Mark. Lizzie began crying just because Mary and Richard were crying.

"You can't go, Mark. Whose gonna take care of us?" cried Mary.

"You still have Mama," Mark replied.

"No we don't!" Mary shot back before she could think. "You know that, too."

If that remark bothered Mama, she didn't show it in the least. She just sat there staring blankly at Mark.

"You know that Uncle Ralph, Uncle Bob, and Uncle Thomas will help out. Uncle Russ, too. Besides, you know how to take care of yourselves. You've been doing it anyway."

"It's just not right, Mark," Mary cried. "This isn't right!"

"Don't be mad, Mary. Hey you guys, don't be sad. I was hoping you'd be happy for me."

"Mark, how can we be happy? Everyone is leaving us." I was angry.

"Pop, you'll be the man of the house when I leave. You'll be in charge. You should like that."

"Yeah, right. I'm ten and a half and I'm supposed to be the man of the house. Uncle Ralph, Uncle Russ, Uncle Thomas, and Uncle Bob have families of their own. How can they take care of us, too?"

We were outnumbered. In a few minutes, Uncle Russ suddenly appeared. I could tell that he and Mark already had discussed this decision. Uncle Russ had been in the Navy during World War I, so he reassured Mama that Mark was doing the right thing for himself. In the Navy, he'd get to travel, finish his education, and could start a career if he wanted to. He reminded her that part of Mark's monthly paycheck could be sent home to help with the bills.

"Uncle Sam will take good care of him. He'll have food,

clothes, and a place to lay his head. Mark will have the opportunity to see places the average person only dreams about seeing in a lifetime." I thought Uncle Russ' speech seemed well-rehearsed. How could anyone possibly know the United States would enter World War II in less than nine months?

Mark was wearing his most pleading look for Mama. "Mama please let me. This is something I really want to do. The recruiter promised that I could earn good money and get my education. I can even stay in the Navy as a career."

Mama, who was sitting in Daddy's leather chair murmured, "I don't know. I just don't know. Russ, what would Randall say? Besides, I'd have to sign for him. Plus, he's only sixteen."

"I think he'd say yes, Iris. I really do," our uncle assured her.

"You're probably right. I think I should talk to Reverend Small, though. He'll have good advice. Mark, we'll wait to see what Reverend Small thinks."

Mark hung his head. "Okay, but I hope he says yes."

Reverend Small again. He'd begun visiting at least once a week, sometimes twice a week if we were extremely unlucky. So the following day, he showed up at Mama's request.

"Hello, Roy," he said in that whiny voice of his. "I've been missing you children in church. I hope to see you Sunday. Is your Mama inside?"

What a dumb question! Of course Mama was inside. That was the only place she ever was. Just like Daddy, Granny – and now, Mark – she had left us a long time ago. I didn't even answer him. I just stepped aside to let him pass.

So because of Reverend Small's advice and blessings, Mark was allowed to join the Navy. Sometime during the night before he was to leave, Mary crept into our room and sat on Mark's side of the bed. I hadn't been able to sleep, but I pretended that I was.

"Mark, are you awake?" She whispered.

"Yeah. I'm too excited to sleep, I guess. What's up?" Mark asked.

"I don't want you to leave." Mary groaned. She started crying. "I'll be lost without you."

"I know. Don't cry, Mary. I can't stand that."

"I can't help it. It's your fault."

"Yeah, I guess it is. You know, I'm gonna miss all of you, too. Did you ever think it might be a little scary for me?"

Mary stopped crying and looked at him. "Probably not. I guess I've been feeling sorry for myself and not thinking about how you feel. Are you going to be okay?"

"Yeah, I'm sure I will. I know I'll get homesick. I always do when I go away anywhere. You'll have to write to me, okay?"

"I will. You know I will." Mary stopped talking and just sat there for the longest time.

"What else is on your mind?"

"Johnny Perkins. I need to ask you something, but promise you won't laugh."

"I won't laugh. Promise. Shoot." Mark gently encouraged her. "Go ahead. What is it?"

"Well, he told Teresa he wanted to kiss me."

"What's wrong with that? At least we know he's not crazy!"

"Well, it scares me." Mary's voice got low.

"Why? Why should it scare you?"

"Be..because, I don't know how." Mary's voice trailed off.

I was having difficulty hearing her.

Mark didn't say anything for what seemed a long time. "Well, it looks like I'll have to show you."

"I don't think so!" Mary giggled. "I'm not about to kiss my own brother on the lips."

"You don't have to. I promise. Here, let me show you how."

"I don't understand!"

"Just follow me."

Mary stood up and Mark rolled out of bed. He grabbed her hand and pulled her to the oak dresser.

"Look in the mirror. Just form your mouth like this, like a little 'o'."

I wanted to laugh but I wouldn't dare, so I strained to watch them in the darkness.

Mark formed his mouth and then pressed his pursed lips onto the mirror. His warm breath and the wetness of his lips left a hazy-looking image on the glass.

"See, it's easy. Now you try."

"I feel stupid."

"Better now than when Johnny Perkins tries," Mark warned.

Mark made a good point. Mary didn't want to be embarrassed, did she? And besides, I was picking up some pointers I would need in the future.

"Mark, where did you learn how to kiss?"

Mark chuckled. "I've been kissing girls since the first grade. I started on the playground at school. Harriet Scott was the first girl I kissed. I've just gotten good at it over the years."

I wasn't shocked. He'd always been a lady's man and popular with the girls.

"You're funny. Well, thanks, Mark. I'll keep practicing."

"Good girl. When it happens, it will come naturally. I promise."

"I hope so." Mary shrugged her shoulders. "Mark?"

"Yeah?"

"Can I kiss you on the cheek?"

"Sure."

Mary pressed a kiss on the side of his face. "I love you."

"Ditto."

After Mary left the room in a hurry, Mark climbed back

into bed. After a few minutes, I heard him sniffling. I had a lump in my throat and wanted to swallow hard, but I was afraid to for fear Mark would hear me. Finally, I fell asleep wishing with all my heart that I wasn't a boy, so I could kiss him, too.

Chapter 28

But he said to me, "My grace is sufficient for you, for my power is made perfect in weakness." Therefore I will boast all the more gladly about my weaknesses, so that Christ's power may rest on me.
2 Corinthians 12:9

Richard: Mark kissed Mama goodbye as she stood on the porch with tears chasing each other down her cheeks.

"Bye, Mama.　Don't worry about me. I'll be fine. I'll write to ya'll and let you know how I'm doing. Love ya, Mama," he said shyly.

"I hope I've done the right thing," she mumbled between her tears.

"You have." He smiled at her.

Mark hugged Mary who was crying into a crumpled tissue. She couldn't talk, but Mark understood. Mark shook hands with Roy, then hugged him quickly. Roy looked uneasy and had tears in his eyes.

"Okay, Pop. You're in charge. Take care of them."

Pop nodded and swallowed hard.

Lee was crying and wiping his nose. He shuffled his weight back and forth from one leg to the other – his old habit. I watched him cram his hands so far into his jean's pockets, I thought his hands would come out the bottom of his pants legs. They embraced. "Help Pop take care of everybody. Don't worry. Keep on growing taller, and you can join the Navy, too."

"Don't give him any ideas," Mama warned with a little laugh.

"Navy?" Lee asked in a mocking voice. "Never. I'm gonna be a fly-boy one day. No ships for me—just the wide blue yonder." Lee nudged Mark's ribs.

When Mark walked over to say goodbye to me, he stopped to ruffle my hair and winked.

"Now, maybe I can git some sleep, bed partner," he

joked.

I thought my heart was going to break into a thousand pieces. The tears began to flow. Mark was really leaving and going far away. We'd shared the double-bed forever. He'd even endured my bed-wetting. Memories flashed through my mind.

So many nights, Mark woke up soaked in pee. He'd wake me up, lift me gently to the floor, and strip the wet sheets from the bed. Then, he'd replace them with clean ones he'd find by rummaging through the dark bathroom linen closet. Patiently, he'd take me back to the bathroom and sit me on the toilet seat. After running warm water into the sink, he'd use a dampened cloth and soap and wash my legs and bottom. Then he'd help me put on new underpants and pajamas and lead me back to bed. Mama and Daddy were never disturbed.

"It's our secret, little buddy. No one has to know," he whispered to me. I only wet the bed on nights when I had dreams that scared me. Finally, I got older and quit doing that, but Mark's patience was what I remembered and would miss. I loved him. First Daddy and now Mark.

Through my tears, I saw him lift Lizzie and swing her around twice. He kissed her on the cheek. He walked over to Tommy who was sitting on the porch with his bottle held tightly in one hand and his blue rattle in the other.

"Bye, little fellow. See you soon." He dangled his finger in front of Tommy who quickly dropped his rattle. Tommy wrapped his tiny fingers around Mark's extended index finger and cooed loudly. Mark shook his finger back and forth, but Tommy held fast. "Yep, you're gonna be a strong one. Pop and Lee better watch out!" Tommy's pink gums and his few teeth appeared as he grinned happily. With one final hug and kiss from Mama, our oldest brother was gone. We watched Uncle Russ's green Buick disappear down the street.

For weeks, we ran to the house every afternoon hoping to find a letter from Mark in the mailbox. Finally, his first letter arrived. In it, he assured us he was all right and enjoying everything so far. Mark was stationed in Maryland and was called a boson's mate. Pop and Lee made jokes that he was a bosom's mate. Mark had included a picture of himself, along with some of his first paycheck.

"He looks so handsome in his white Navy uniform," Mary said.

"Don't you think he looks a lot older in it?" Mama asked.

"Yeah, he does. You're right. I'm glad he's happy," Mary replied. "Can I take the picture to school, Mama, and show it to the other girls?"

"Yeah, but just be careful it doesn't get bent. Richard, did you see your brother's picture?"

When I looked at the picture, I gasped loudly. I think all the blood in my body ran to my feet. It was like seeing a ghost.

"Richard? Are you okay?" Mama seemed alarmed.

"Yes ma'am. I'm okay." I couldn't stand it. I ran out of the living room to our bedroom and laid across the bed. I suddenly needed to read my new Bible – the one I'd gotten for Christmas.

"Hey, Richard!" Pop followed me into the room. "Are you okay?"

"Yeah. I just want to read my Bible." I tried to act normal.

"You're not reading anything. You're just looking at the pictures," Pop observed. Then he plopped down beside me.

"I know. You're right."

"Why did you turn white when you looked at Mark's picture?"

"I don't want to talk about it, right now, Roy, I mean Pop."

"You don't have to call me Pop all the time. Anyway, why don't you want to talk?"

"Pop. Please just leave me alone right now and let me

think."

"No. I don't want to leave you alone. I want you to tell me what's wrong." Roy could be a pain at times.

"Okay, then." I was exasperated. "If you have to know, it's my fault Mark joined the Navy."

"What do ya mean it's your fault?" he asked. "That's not true."

"I dreamed it. That's why he left. I dreamed it. If I hadn't dreamed it, it wouldn't have happened. My dreams always happen. They always come true."

Roy looked puzzled. "Your dream isn't why he left, Richard. He left because he wanted to join the Navy. He left because he wanted to. No dream could make it happen."

"Maybe. But I dream things, and then they come true. Roy, I even dreamed about you breaking your ankle. Then you did!"

"You did? Why didn't you tell me?" Roy's eyes were big.

"Cause I didn't want to scare you."

"Why not? You could have saved me a lot of pain and time in a cast." He was laughing. "What else have you dreamed about? Wait a minute. Do I really want to know?"

I hesitated. "Daddy. I dreamed about Daddy getting sick. Then, he did get sick. See? See why I think it's my fault. I've dreamed about other things, too. I dreamed about Granny the other night, and I keep dreaming about all of us playing in a big yard."

"Anybody want to play me in a game of checkers?" Lee yelled from the other room. "Richard? Pop?"

Roy ignored Lee. "What about Granny and the dream about us?" He was curious.

"I don't remember," I mumbled.

"Pop? You better c'mon. I've got the board set up. I'm ready to win tonight," Lee interrupted again.

"The dreams aren't bad, I don't think," I assured him. "In the dream, we're playing. We're okay. There are other kids around and lots of buildings."

"Maybe we're going on a trip somewhere. Who knows?" Roy was distracted by the promise of a game of checkers. "Lee, I'll be there in a second. Richard, you can tell me more about your dreams later. All right?"

"Yeah. But promise me you won't tell anybody what I told you."

"Promise. Our secret." Then he jumped off the bed and disappeared into the other room.

Chapter 29

*Our obligation is to give meaning to life and in doing so to overcome
the passive, indifferent life.*
Elie Wiesel

Roy: It wasn't long before Mary started fixing breakfast and supper for us. We all pitched in and cleaned the house and washed the clothes on Saturdays. Since Granny left, I'd taken over most of the ironing. Actually, I was getting pretty good at it. Lee sometimes complained about having to wash the dishes every night, but I think it was just frustration and a way of venting. Richard never complained about having to do anything. He was a big help by playing with Lizzie and Tommy who now was walking and getting into everything. Yeah, our lives were a barrel of fun. What other kids were having this much fun?

One Saturday afternoon when Lizzie was helping Mary feed the wet clothes through the rollers of the washing machine, we heard a piercing scream coming from the kitchen. Mary came running into the living room where we were, holding her head and screaming.

"Pop! Come quick. It's Lizzie! Hurry!"

I ran into the kitchen where Lizzie was standing on a kitchen chair with her little arm elbow-deep through the rollers. The washing machine was slowly devouring Lizzie. Hurriedly, I jerked the electric plug from the wall and popped the latch over the top of the two rollers. Immediately, her arm was released. Gratefully, I pulled her free. Then, she began to cry. Mary examined her arm carefully. It didn't appear to be broken. Lizzie was just scared to death by all the excitement and commotion. Mama appeared in the doorway to inquire about Lizzie.

"What's wrong?"

"Nothin'. Everything is fine," I stressed in an authoritative tone.

She seemed convinced and returned to her bedroom. I just shook my head in disgust.

Everyone's school work began to suffer – that is except for Richard's. After all, first grade was no sweat, anyway. Just a bunch of check marks and minuses. Up until this school year, Mary had been a straight "A" student. I'd gotten tired of my idol, Miss Greene, keeping me behind during recess so that she could pry details from me. She seemed really interested in our personal lives. I was wary and became tight-lipped. Besides, I was becoming paranoid thinking it was Miss Greene sending Reverend Small to our house all the time. Even though I liked her looks and perfume, I didn't want to marry her anymore. I'd decided I didn't want to get married. Ever!

One day in May before school was out for the summer, Mary was sick with a headache and stayed home. That afternoon, she met our bus at the stop sign. She looked worried about something. I noticed Russell Thomas giving her the eye, and that bothered me. Russell caught me watching him and smirked. I ignored him. I was more concerned about Mary.

"Pop, I've got to talk to you," she whispered. This seemed urgent so it piqued my curiosity.

"Lee, you and Richard run ahead. I need to talk to Mary," I suggested.

"Okay. Are we gonna play football?" Lee asked.

"Maybe, after we finish any chores," I replied.

After they ran towards the house, I turned to Mary. "Okay. What's up?"

"Well, I don't really know. But, Reverend Small was visiting today."

"What? That's not news. I don't know why he doesn't pack his bags and move on in. If he ain't in the pulpit preaching hell fire and damnation and spitting all over the people in the front row, he's spitting all over our floor."

"Yeah. I know. Well, anyway, let me finish. Mama and the Reverend were talking low 'cause Mama thought I was asleep. I kept hearing them say a word over and over again."

"What word?" I asked.

Mary held her breath. "Orphanage. Roy, Mama can't be thinking about putting us in an orphanage can she?"

"What is it?"

"You know. A place for kids who don't have parents or a home."

"Oh." My stomach turned somersaults. I decided to logically think this through. "Okay, we have a parent, right?"

"Yes."

"We have a home, right?"

"Yes."

I began convincing myself. "Then we don't fit the definition. We have a parent and a home, so that can't be what they were talking about."

"Yeah, but why would they be talking about it? Why would they be using that word?" Mary insisted.

"I don't know. Besides, you know how strange Reverend Small is. He's always talking about stupid things. But you're right. There's no telling what he's saying to Mama. At least she talks to him. She definitely doesn't talk to us anymore."

"Well, it scares me. Should I call Granny?"

"No! Not yet. Not until we know more. And we sure don't wanna tell Lee or Richard. Let's jest keep our ears and eyes open. Deal?"

"Okay, deal," she said reluctantly. She wasn't totally convinced I was right. I wasn't either.

"Besides, Mary. Grandma and Granny and Uncle Russ and Uncle Ron and all the others wouldn't let that happen to us. Would they?"

"No. Probably, not. You're right. That is, I hope you're right," she said.

"Well, we need to pray that I'm right. We'll jest be careful and keep our eyes open. If we learn it might be true, we'll write to Mark. He'll stop it. Mark wouldn't let anything happen to us - not in a million years."

When we reached the porch steps, Lee came crashing through the front door. He was crying.

"Oh, my God, Pop! It's Granny. She's dead."

Chapter 30

Those who hope in the Lord will renew their strength. They will soar on wings like eagles; they will run and not grow weary, they will walk and not be faint.
Isaiah 40:31

Richard: Our sadness didn't stop with Mark leaving. Just a few weeks later, we got the news that Granny had died. Somehow, when she left to return home to Charlotte, I knew I wouldn't ever see her again. Something inside just told me so, and I had dreamed it – many times.

In my recurring dream, Granny was sitting on a white puffy cloud and floating high into the air. She was waving and blowing kisses to me.

"Granny. You be careful! You might fall," I cried. Actually, I was afraid she'd fall through the cloud.

"It's beautiful from up here. It's so quiet, too," she called. Granny's face was peaceful. She actually looked younger, radiant, and her smile was so sweet.

"Where are you going?" I asked.

"I'm going to Heaven. One day, you'll come, too, and we'll be together again. I promise."

Because of her delight, I didn't ask her to come back even though my heart was shouting it. Granny was leaving us, too. So instead, I just shouted to the disappearing figure. "I'll miss you so bad!"

"Remember," she shouted back, "it won't be long, lad. It won't be long. Granny loves ya. Be happy for me. It's so peaceful where I'm goin."

When the billowy white cloud disappeared behind the golden sun, I awoke with my head buried in my tear-soaked pillow. Not, Granny. That was the dream I chose not to think about or dwell on for fear it would come true. She was right – I didn't always like my special gift.

Our hearts were broken when Mama told us she didn't

feel up to making the trip to Charlotte, and she certainly wasn't going to take five children and a baby on a lengthy train trip. Even Grandma tried to change her mind.

"Iris, you really should go and pay your respects. After all, she was Randall's mother. I'll keep the children with me. Besides, a change of scenery might be good for you. I'm worried about you never leaving this house. You don't go anywhere anymore. The kids say you stay in bed most of the time."

"Mama, I can't help it. I just don't feel good anymore."

"Well, I think you should go. A few days away, even if it is for Anna's funeral, might just do you some good. Anyway, what will Randall's family think if you don't go? Ron and Russ have been good to you and the children. I'm sure you could go to Charlotte with them and not have to ride a train."

"I don't feel like a trip. They'll be leaving early to make the arrangements. And I really don't care what anyone thinks."

She was adamant not to go. "Don't you think people will understand what I'm going through? Here I am with a house full of kids and bills to pay. I've got to find a job. That's going to be interesting since I've never had a job."

"I understand, Iris. You have a lot on your shoulders, but I think going would be the responsible thing to do."

"I don't care. I don't care about doing the responsible thing." She pounded her fist on the melamine table. "Mama, it's only been a few months since he died. I just can't face another funeral so soon. Besides, it'd be him all over again since she's his mother. The same people would be there, crying their eyes out. I can't take it!" Tears pooled in Mama's eyes and spilled over onto her cheeks.

Grandma threw her hands up in the air and gave up. Her advice was useless. Mama wasn't going to the funeral and neither were we. We loved Granny, and we wanted to say goodbye to her. There had to be a way to see her one more time. Then I remembered Mrs. Johnson.

"Mrs. Johnson? Would it be okay if I picked one of your red roses?"

"Of course, you can, dear. Is it for your mama?"

"No ma'am," I replied.

"Then, who is it for, sweetie? A little girlfriend?" she asked with a cheery smile.

"Naw! It's for Granny. Granny died yesterday, and Mama said we're not goin' to her funeral because she don't feel like it."

"Oh, Richard. I'm so sorry to hear this. I liked your Granny very much," she said softly. "She was a wonderful person."

"I know. She was. So, I'm trying to think of something special to do for Granny. Since we can't go there, I want to do something here, so Granny'll know we love her."

"I'm sure your Granny already knows that." Then she remembered my request.

"Here, let me help you get a rose." Mrs. Johnson went inside to grab her black scissors from her sewing basket. When she returned, she leaned over the creaking wooden railing and cut the prettiest blossom from her climbing red rose bush.

"Richard, would you like more than one?"

"No, ma'am. Just one. Granny liked the song, 'Just One Rose Will Do'."

"Then, here, darling. You're so thoughtful, aren't you? Always thinking of someone else. You're a special little boy."

Mrs. Johnson waved to me as I walked towards the old oak tree—the same one where Daddy had buried the treasure box. We'd adopted this as our special place.

I sat under its huge boughs and looked up though the dense limbs at the fluffy clouds. I recalled my vivid dream about Granny. Then, I thought about the ghost stories. No more ghost stories or ever seeing her come down the street towards our home. No more smiles – she was always smil-ing. She was so sad at Daddy's funeral, but she had found a way to smile. And she had come to help me and my family afterwards. We'd worn her out. Bible stories. No more reading the Bible to Granny. As my thoughts built into huge mounds of grief, I couldn't hold back the tears. I flung myself down on the hard, protruding roots of the ancient tree and cried my heart out for what seemed to be hours. When at last I felt drained and weak, I placed the rose gently on the ground.

"Granny, this is for you," I said with my head bowed.

May the road rise up to meet you,
May the wind be always at your back,
May the sunshine be warm upon your face,
May the rain fall soft upon your fields,
And until we meet again,
May God hold you in the hollow of his hand.

And I added, *"May the clouds always be white and fluffy wherever you are."*

This was my simple way of honoring Granny.

Chapter 31

To be nobody-but-yourself – in a world which is doing its best, night and day, to make you everybody but yourself – means to fight the hardest battle which any human being can fight and never stop fighting.
e. e. cummings

Roy: We were devastated when Granny died. And to add to our sadness, Mama decided we weren't going to the funeral. None of us. That really made me mad. A few days after the funeral, Aunt Jeannie telephoned to check on us. She talked with Mary for a long time, filling her in on all the details. Afterwards, Mary shared the conversation with us, including Mama.

"Aunt Jeannie said there were hundreds of people at her funeral. I'm not exaggerating, hundreds," Mary started.

We didn't doubt that. Granny was loved by everyone who knew her.

"She got lots of flowers, too. Actually, there were so many wreaths of flowers, they covered her grave and spread over five others on either side."

That would have made Granny happy because she loved beautiful flowers just like she loved people.

Mary continued. "Granny was buried in her favorite green dress with her Bible in her hands."

"All that sounds nice. It sounds like Mother Anna had a good send off," Mama quietly replied.

Even though she couldn't read a lick, she'd worn her black Bible out just holding it all the time and flipping its pages. Well, maybe she could read now, in Heaven. I pictured her sitting on a cloud with lots of little kids around her reading them Bible stories. She was sure to have angel's wings, too, big and fluffy and white. I bet she was standing at those pearly gates Reverend Small talked about all the time, reciting any verses God wanted to hear. If so, she was probably giving

Saint Peter lots of company.

At the end of the school year, we all passed our grades. Richard finished the first grade by receiving lots of 'Ss' for satisfactory and some "S pluses", too. Mine and Lee's grades weren't that good; I'd struggled this year in the fourth grade. Even Mary, the straight "A" student, got more "Bs" and "Cs" to end her sixth school year. Mama didn't seem to notice. Just like during the school year when I'd gotten into lots of fights and ended up being paddled several times by Mr. Gardner. He sent disciplinary notes home to Mama to inform her I'd been causing "havoc," but Mama never received those notes. I made sure of that. Somehow, I'd been able to convince Mary to sign Mama's name on the bottom of each note. Actually, it surprised me that Mary would do such a dishonest thing, but she became my friend, my confidant. We learned quickly to rely on each other. But I often wondered why Mama didn't question my black eyes or torn clothes.

Lee had changed, too. Never talking much, staying to himself, staying under the crawl space. He was never interested in playing marbles or cars or horse races. He just sat and thought, which was unlike Lee. The crawlspace became his little haven. Lee didn't even seem interested in girls anymore. The little "ladies' man," the one who always tried to steal a kiss from some pretty girl on the school playground or neighborhood, wasn't interested. He didn't even play his favorite trick anymore, the one where he'd get a girl to bend over and pick up a ball so he could see her underpants. We were changed.

We did have one bright light in our dark world. Mark's letters usually arrived once a week—on Tuesday or Wednesday—so we eagerly anticipated their arrivals. Mama seemed excited to get them, too. She read them to us after supper. Mark was a good writer. He shared stories about his adventures, described his many Navy buddies, wrote about his job duties as a boson's mate, and mentioned tidbits of the war going on in Europe. These serial letters became the highlight of our weeks. In one letter each month, we'd get some of his monthly check.

After reading the letters, Mama would stumble back to the kitchen to drink coffee or into her bedroom to read or to sleep or to just stare at Daddy's picture. She never laughed, never touched our faces, and never told us that she loved us. Mama had become a stranger existing in our house but living in a different world.

Then when things couldn't get much worse, Reverend Small began visiting Mama at least two or three times each week, always bringing an apple pie that Martha or one of the other Presbyterian ladies had made. Always telling us he missed our smiling faces at church. What smiling faces?

Shortly after his visits increased, Mama declared a new rule concerning the mail.

"From now one, I'm the only one who'll get the mail out of the mailbox," she said. "I don't want any of you to bother getting the mail. Let me do it."

"Why?" I asked. I was beginning to resent the authority that she never exercised any other time.

"Because I said so, that's why. It's as simple as that," she said.

Mary and I looked at each other. Something was wrong. That's when I stopped sleeping or thinking about anything other than trying to figure out what was going on. Paranoia grabbed me by the throat and wouldn't let go of its tight grip.

One night, Richard awoke from a dream. When he found my bed empty, he panicked and searched the dark rooms. Finally, he peered out the backdoor window and saw me in the backyard. He startled me as I was bent over the scorched barrel searching through charred tin cans and bottles and reading bits of paper with a flashlight.

"Roy? Roy? What are ya doin?" He whispered loudly.

I jerked my head up and peered at him in the moonlight. Richard stopped cold. He didn't say a word. Finally, he asked again.

"Pop? What are ya doin?" He was nervous.

I'm sure I looked wild, like I was a hungry animal or something searching the trash for a morsel. I thought I'd just found out what the morsel was. My jaws twitched as I drew my lips together and clinched my fists. I'm sure Richard thought I was going to hit him. He seemed to brace himself. That hurt me because I'd never hit him and never would.

"Richard, why are you out here snooping around after me? Ya need to git your little butt back to bed and leave me alone," I said too gruffly.

"I had a dream. When I woke up, you were gone. I just wanted...."

He didn't finish his sentence, and I didn't pursue it. I couldn't take another one of his dreams.

I said more softly, "Well, go back to bed. I'm okay. I'll be there soon."

When Richard teared up, I wanted to cry myself. I was scared, embarrassed. My heart was beating out of my chest. I wanted to run like a scared rabbit until I was safely hid under the wrinkled sheets in our bed. More than anything, I wished Mark was here. Richard sat quietly with me for about thirty minutes while I gathered my thoughts and emotions. Then we crept up the steps of the back porch and turned the squeaky door-knob. Tired and emotionally drained, we eased ourselves into the bedroom where Lee was sleeping soundly. After Richard climbed into his empty bed, I tiptoed over and touched his hair. He flinched.

"Richard?" I whispered. "You know I'd never hurt ya. I've got a lot on my mind, so will you say a prayer for me, for us?"

"Sure. What about?"

"I don't know. Make up somethin'. Anything will do."

"Okay. I will right now before I go back to sleep."

"Good. Thanks!" I tiptoed back to bed and climbed

in, careful not to disturb Lee who now was snoring loudly. I punched him so he'd turn over off his back, and he did.

After we ate breakfast and washed the dishes the next moring, Mary and I hurried out the door.

"I'll be back in a little while to help clean up, Mama," Mary called to the open bedroom door where Mama was still lying in bed.

Richard and Lee were playing with Tommy, while Lizzie was pouting about something. Who knew what? This would buy us some time. We hurried down the road towards the stop sign before heading to the oak tree where I started pacing. Mary sat patiently and waited for me to speak.

If anyone had been listening, they would have heard my voice alternate between soft and loud. They would have seen Mary cover her face with her hands and start crying. They would have seen her shoulders shaking and me standing there not knowing what to do until I sat on the ground and cradled my own head between my knees. We stayed in our temporary sanctuary and let the pain and confusion flow until both our eyes were red, and we couldn't stand to be there any longer.

When we returned home, we found everyone outside under the house. I apologized to Richard.

"Hey, sorry about last night, okay?"

"Okay." He shrugged his little shoulders. "No problem."

"Are ya sure? I don't want ya to be mad at me," I asked.

"Yeah, I'm sure."

"What about last night?" Lee asked, suddenly aware of our existence.

"Nothin'," I said quickly. "Man! Can't I even have a conversation around here without someone else having to know?"

"Don't fight. I don't feel like anyone fighting today," Mary injected. She looked fragile, just like I felt. I definitely wasn't up to a fight. Lee went back to drawing pictures in the dirt. Lizzie was curled up on her side, asleep. We stayed under the house that morning where it was cool and provided a safe haven. Around lunchtime, we heard the sound of Reverend Small's car pull into the driveway.

"What's he doin' here again?" I asked no one in particular while crossing my arms defensively. I made a circle in the dirt with my big toe. "I'm just tired of him bein' here all the time. You know why he's here."

Mary looked quickly in my direction.

"I know, but we can't talk about it now. Not now." Her eyes were daggers warning me to be quiet. She crawled out from under the house and disappeared down the road in the direction of Mrs. Johnson's house.

"Roy, what's goin' on? I'm tired of you and Mary acting weird all the time. Tell me what it is," Lee said. He was picking his nose.

"You're disgusting, Lee. Stop that!" I yelled to shame him. "Besides, I don't really know what's goin' on."

Richard and Lee knew I wasn't telling the truth because I couldn't stare them in the eyes when I talked.

"I've got my hunches, but I don't know for sure. Shush! Listen!" I cautioned them.

Above our heads, we could hear the muffled voices of Mama and Reverend Small. As we listened intently, we could pick out words or phrases but rarely sentences. Then, we heard footsteps pacing back and forth in the living room.

"I'm hungry," moaned Lizzie as she awakened.

"Quiet, Lizzie," I whispered. She must have known I meant it because she didn't make another whimper.

After another child's eternity, Reverend Small stepped onto the porch.

"I'll be back in touch, Iris. We'll need to decide quickly."

"I know," she said quietly. "I do know that. I could never do this alone, so thank you for all your help and advice."

"God bless you, Iris. You and the children are in my prayers."

"Please tell Martha I said hello."

"I will. Bye."

A few minutes after we watched his car disappear down the road for the last time, I hoped, Mama yelled for us to come into lunch. She'd stacked triangular tomato sandwiches, peanut butter and jelly sandwiches, and pimento cheese sandwiches on a plate in the middle of the kitchen table. There was fresh lemonade made with the lemons Mrs. Thomas brought to us. Mama actually smiled at us as we plopped into the vinyl chairs surrounding the table. Had she been crying? I couldn't tell. I couldn't remember when her eyes weren't red-rimmed or shiny with tears.

"Eat up. I have things to do," she said. Her voice was firm. In other words, we were supposed to hurry up and eat and get back outside where the doors would be locked behind us.

"Where's Mary?" she asked. She'd finally noticed one of us was missing.

"At Mrs. Johnson's, I think," I said in between the bites I was forcing myself to eat. I motioned in the direction of Mrs. Johnson's house.

"What's she doing down there?" Mama asked. Was she angry? It was hard to tell.

I wiped a dab of mayonnaise from the corner of my mouth. "I dunno. She just went down there without really sayin' anything."

Mama looked out the kitchen window towards Mrs. Johnson's house. She picked up Tommy and put him in the wooden high chair where he started feeding himself mashed peas from last night's supper. "What have ya'll been doing this morning?" Was she trying to make small talk, or was she being nosey?

Richard answered her. "Just playin' under the house."

"Did ya'll see Reverend Small?" she asked coyly.

"Yes ma'am," we replied in unison.

"I bet you can hear lots of stuff when you're under the house. Richard, what kinds of things do ya'll hear?"

"Not much really. Just footsteps, mostly."

Good boy.

"Roy, is that true? All you hear are footsteps? Don't you hear me talking on the phone or to Tommy or Reverend Small when he comes to visit?"

"Nothin'. Jest footsteps. That's all," I lied.

She didn't seem convinced, but she continued feeding Tommy who was squealing like a little pig and making all of us smile. After lunch, we took turns using the bathroom and ran outside to play. Again, the door was locked behind us. Mary never came home for lunch and stayed down at Mrs. Johnson's most of the afternoon. When she did come home, she was calm. I bet Mrs. Johnson had fed her more than just chocolate-chip cookies.

Chapter 32

As a father has compassion on his children, so the Lord has compassion on those who fear him; for he knows how we are formed, he remembers that we are dust.
Psalm 103: 13-14

Richard: We played outside until Mama called us in for supper. We ate quickly and ran outside to get in a game of hide-n-seek with the neighborhood kids. I noticed Johnny Perkins and Mary seemed to always be coming from the same direction. Maybe they were hiding together. It was obvious that Johnny had a crush on Mary. Evidently, it was mutual. After all, Mary would soon be fourteen in October; Johnny already was fourteen. Johnny's appearance was a contrast to Mary's. Johnny had blonde, curly hair and the brightest green eyes. Johnny had a part-time job this summer working in the hardware store four blocks away. I noticed that whenever Johnny whispered something in Mary's ear, she'd blush and giggle. Mary acted differently when she was around Johnny. It was fun to watch her.

My older brothers were masters at hide-n-seek. They had the best hiding places possible. Sometimes Lee would climb a tree or crawl behind the oil drum behind the house. Either way, they could run fast enough to beat most "it" kids back to "home base."

"Me wanna play, too," Lizzie cried. "Me wanna play hide seat."

"Does she have to?" Lee asked.

"Yeah. She can play," I said. "C'mon Lizzie. You can hide with me." There wasn't much of a chance I'd never get caught. I'd be "it" for the rest of the night. Then Johnny came to my rescue.

"Naw, Richard. She can come with us," motioning towards Mary. Mary blushed because in his innocence to help, he'd drawn attention to them being together.

"I wanna go with John John!" Lizzie cried.

Johnny always liked to play with Lizzie because she was "so cute and darling." Johnny didn't have a little sister, so he couldn't imagine how demanding she could be. I was thankful for the break.

After we tired of playing hide-n-seek, we split up into two teams and found two mason jars in Daddy's shed.

"Okay, each team has thirty minutes to catch lightning bugs. Whoever has the most at the end of thirty minutes wins," Roy declared.

"We already know who that's gonna be," shouted Russell Thomas.

"Yeah?" asked Roy. "And who is that?"

"Need you ask? My team of course," Russell replied. Somehow, he and Roy always ended up on opposite teams. I wondered if that was a blessing or a curse.

I made sure I was on Pop and Lee's team and not on Russell's. After the cookie incident, I didn't like being around him. After we divided into two equal teams, we rushed around nearby yards in pursuit of yellow sparks. Some of the adults rocked or swung in their porch swings. As we grabbed at the elusive flying bugs, we heard soft chuckles and low murmuring talk.

Even Mama ventured outside to watch. I thought she looked pretty sitting on the top porch step hugging her knees like she used to do when Daddy was here. At the end of what Russell called thirty minutes, both teams gathered in the Thomas' yard to count the little prisoners. To make it fair, Mr. Thomas counted the bugs – just like Daddy used to do.

"Fifteen for Russell's team! Seventeen for Roy's!" He exclaimed. "Roy, looks like your team wins!"

Mrs. Johnson met us at the end of the Thomas' driveway with a fresh batch of oatmeal and raisin cookies. These were a welcome treat!

"Everyone, get a cookie," Mrs. Johnson cooed. After we all had fists full of the warm and pliable creation, Mrs.

Johnson gathered us around.

"Children, may I ask a favor of you? Will you let the little bugs go so they don't smother in the jars? If you do, you can probably catch them again on another night. How about it? What do you think?"

Those were Daddy's words. "If you let 'em go, then you can catch 'em tomorrow night." I could almost hear him saying it. Mrs. Johnson didn't have to plead with us. Russell and Roy unscrewed the jar lids and laid the jars sideways on the ground. One by one, they escaped into the night air, like tiny dancing stars close enough to touch.

An hour or so later, we climbed into our beds and closed tired eyes. We'd all dream about catching lightning bugs tonight. That is, maybe everyone but me. I dreamed another one of my recurring dreams again that night.

"You're going to like it here, Richard. This is a very special place for very special children," a plump, elderly lady said to me. She reminded me of Granny with her white hair and green eyes. She had gold wire-rimmed glasses, too. But she wasn't Granny. "There are lots of children here. They're always playing games."

"But I really want to be at home with my family," I insisted.

"We'll take good care of you here," she said. "And, best of all, you'll be with him. He lives here." I wondered who he was. Who did she mean? It looked like a nice place, but I was homesick.

"Where's Pop? Where's Mary and Lizzie? Is Lee and Tommy here, too?" I was looking all around me. But we were alone.

"Do you know where Mark is?"

She smiled at me, lowered her glasses, and replied, "Sure. They're not here yet, but they're coming. You'll find this is a wonderful and most desirable place."

"Will we go home sometime?"

"After you're here for a short while, I promise you

won't even want to go home again." The lady's voice was really calming and peaceful. It had a lovely gay sound, like a flute.

But I started crying.

"Don't cry. We'll make you happy. Come with me, and I'll show you." When she turned around, I was shocked.

"You're an angel!" I gasped. Her wings were tucked, but I could see they were white and bordered with silver, glittering edging.

"So are you!" She laughed.

I awoke relieved to be in my bed. No angels, no lady in a black dress, nothing out of the normal. I lay listening to my brothers snoring softly in the next bed. I watched the hovering shadows until the morning light chased them away. Then I slept. This became another recurring dream that lasted a long time.

Chapter 33

We cannot escape fear. We can only transform it into a companion that accompanies us on all our exciting adventures...Take a risk a day-any small or bold stroke that will make you feel great once you have done it.
Susan Jeffers

Roy: I heard Reverend Small's black car early that Monday morning in the summer I'd like to forget. When I heard the car's roaring engine become a hissing hiccup, I pulled back the living room curtains to greet him with a sneer. How I'd grown to dislike the sight of this man! He just sat there motionless behind the massive round steering wheel in the front seat of the old Plymouth. His head was bowed as if he were praying. He needed to pray for forgiveness because he'd never get that from me.

I felt dehydrated from all the secret crying I'd done over the past few days. Mary, Lee, and even Richard, hadn't hidden their feelings. They'd cried loudly, pounded their fists, promised all kinds of things, and begged, begged, begged. This was unbearable but obviously true. My eyes were so swollen they looked like I'd been in the worst fight of my life.

Funny. Maybe I was, but I was losing.

Mary and I had had our suspicions, but now, our dreaded fears were coming true. This was hard to comprehend now just like it had been three days ago when Mama made her announcement, the worst news I'd ever heard – even over the news about Daddy and Granny and Mark. This was hard.

Mama had signed the papers to place us in an orphanage over 300 miles away from our home on Mercy Avenue. We would no longer live here; we'd live in a place with a lot of other kids. Kids who had no parents. Kids who had no homes. Kids who had nowhere to go. Somehow, now we fit the last criteria.

I kept thinking, "This had to be a nightmare, and I'm

going to wake up any minute." But I didn't.

Then I kept waiting for the prankster, Uncle Bob, to break into a big toothy grin, chuckling in his low deep-throated way and declare this a big joke. I'd even forgive him if it were. I looked over at his tall, lanky frame sitting in the middle of the sofa. He was holding his balding head in his hands, and they were trembling. I thought he was crying. He kept shaking his head back and forth. Mama sat quietly in Daddy's chair and dabbed at (artificial?) tears in the corners of her brown, lifeless eyes. She stared off in the distance, away from the searching eyes of her children.

Mama chose my favorite night of the week to make her plans known. She'd fixed a delicious meal of fried chicken, mashed potatoes, crowder peas, and homemade biscuits. I should have known something was wrong. She kept looking at the wall-mounted clock. When Reverend Small and Uncle Bob suddenly appeared at the door at 7:00, they ruined our planned game of hide-n-seek after supper. All the kids were supposed to meet in the Thomas' yard at 8:00. Mama greeted them at the door then called us into the living room where Reverend Small suggested we begin with prayer. No sir. This wasn't going to be good. I was sure when he reached over with his short, stubby fingers to still Mama's clenched hands that were visibly shaking. Even her knuckles were white.

"Dear, dear heavenly Father. We thank you for this time when we can gather in a God-fearing home to do your will. We thank you for these dear children, for Iris, and for Bob. We are grateful for the many blessings we've taken for granted today. Tonight, we especially need your guidance. We beseech your help in finding the right words of explanation. We pray for those involved to be comforted and to find peace in things that will soon take place. We pray that your will be done in each of these young lives and in our lives. Thank you for opening new doors and creating new paths. Again, we pray for your strength and guidance in all that we do. In Christ's name we pray. Amen."

My eyes had been open the whole time. I watched Reverend Small turn to Mama. "Iris, do you want to begin?"

"I guess." Mama whispered. She looked nervous and hesitated. He squeezed her hand to give her strength.

We waited for what seemed to be an eternity before she started speaking. I looked around the room. We all looked miserable. Lizzie and Tommy were missing. Mama conveniently had taken them to Mrs. Johnson's house after supper. Mrs. Johnson was going to baby-sit for an hour or two, so we could talk, mama had informed us. When she cleared her voice, I knew this was really, really bad.

"Children, there is something I need to tell you. Something that I've decided. Before I do, I want you to know how much I love each one of you." She paused, wiped her eyes, and continued. "I've prayed about this every day for a long time, so I hope you'll understand this wasn't something I decided quickly. I've talked to Reverend Small, and he's been very helpful to me. I appreciate his advice and his guidance so much." She turned and smiled at him. "It's my deepest hope that someday you'll understand how much this hurts me. I'm convinced there is no better answer." She stopped to blow her nose. "One day, you'll come to see why this is the right thing for all of us."

Mary's and my eyes locked. We just stared at each other and dreaded the next words. Reverend Small nodded silently, encouraging her to continue. Uncle Bob just stared. She pulled a white tissue from the front pocket of her green and white cotton housedress.

"You all know how hard it's been since your daddy died. He didn't leave us with a lot of money. With him being sick and in the sanitarium, he didn't get to work so we didn't have his paycheck. The funeral cost a lot of money. I had to use some of our savings for that. Mark's Navy checks have helped us, but what he sends just isn't enough to keep us going. I've never worked outside the home, but I have to get a job to support ...."

She began rambling about something. A job? I can't remember. I was waiting to hear the awful words.

"I don't know what type of job I can get. I know there is something I can do, but I don't know what that might be. I probably won't make a lot of money." She stopped talking to cry softly into the tissue.

"Go ahead, Iris. You have to go ahead." Reverend Small urged her to continue.

Her voice quivered. "What I'm trying to say—Reverend Small helped me make a decision. It's a hard decision. I believe you children should go to live somewhere else. I don't believe I can make enough money to support all of us. I'm scared we won't have food and clothes. I don't know if I can keep the house. You will need shoes, clothes, and food. I want you to have toys and other things that you want. You're such good kids and so deserving. I want you to have happy lives. You're going to live in an orphanage, for a little while, that is." She turned to Reverend Small. "I can't say anymore. I don't know what else to say."

No one did. We were speechless, too.

Then Richard broke the silence with a child's innocent question. "What's an orphanage?"

Mama began sobbing so Reverend Small leaned forward and firmly grasped her trembling shoulders. Our uncle sat motionless. Mary had that "I told you so" look. So our worst fears had come true. We'd suspected it for months. Huge elephant tears streamed down all our faces leaving weird little paths on our skin. I felt anger, fear, hatred, disbelief, disgust, sadness, pity, shock – everything but love. Richard covered his wet eyes with both hands and hung his head. Every now and then, he wiped his forehead and brushed his hair from his face. His little shoulders shook, so I knew he was crying for all of us.

I heard an angry voice from somewhere deep inside me. "Well, I'm not going. We're not going, and you're not gonna make us." I directed my anger and disgust to Reverend

Small. "Who are you to make decisions for us? You're not kin to us. I don't want you making any decisions for us. You're nobody!"

Uncle Bob nodded his head in support.

"Well, I've looked the word up in the dictionary. Orphanages are for kids who don't have parents. Well, we're not orphans! We have a mama, and we have a home. Daddy never would've put us in an orphanage if you'd been the one to die. And on top of that, he wouldn't have wanted you to do it either."

Mama looked like I'd slapped her.

My body was shaking from head to toe with nerves. My skinny legs felt like spaghetti. I didn't think they'd support me too much longer. My arms hung by my sides; both fists were clenched in rage. Then I defiantly raised my right fist to Reverend Small. He sat forward on the couch. Mama, who had stopped crying, looked hard at me, maybe for the first time in a long time. Was I a stranger to her like she was to me? Who was this woman who now stretched out her arms to me. There was nothing I wanted from her anymore – except a change in this decision. I backed towards the kitchen.

"Roy! Roy! Please calm down, son," she pleaded.

"Calm down!" I shouted. "You calm down! How can you do this to us? Who are you?" I was crying now, and I didn't care. "How can you do this? You're our mother!" Maybe if I shouted it enough, she'd remember. I demanded answers because I was fighting for my life.

"Roy. Please calm down, son. You're making this harder. This decision wasn't easy for your mother to make. You're upsetting your brothers and sister. Please try to calm down and let's talk rationally about this. We'll answer your questions. Now, sit down, son, and let's talk," Reverend Small said extending his open palms.

"Roy's not the one upsetting us," Mary said calmly. "You and Mama are upsetting us."

"Well, I'm sorry, Mary. We had to tell you," Reverend

Small replied.

"No, you didn't have to tell us," Mary said. "You didn't have to make this decision."

Lee and Richard were still crying.

"Haven't our lives changed enough this past year? What else is going to happen to us? We didn't cause any of this – not for Daddy to get sick, for him to die, for Granny to die, for Mark to join the Navy. Don't you understand? Our lives are hard. Mama never talks to us, hardly acts like we're around. She doesn't care what grades we make or even if we go to school. Sometimes I wonder if she even cares if we're alive." Mary's litany rang true and was beautiful to my ears.

"Mary! That's a horrible thing to say. Of course your mother cares. It's because she cares she's doing this."

I couldn't believe my ears! I was convinced Reverend Small was the first to mention this crazy idea to Mama. Somehow, he'd brainwashed her.

Uncle Bob stood. "I certainly understand how they feel. This is a hard thing for a bunch of kids to be told. It's hard for me to sit hear and listen to it. I don't agree with it. Iris, I told you we'd help in any way we could. I'm going home. This is making me sick. Children, Uncle Bob loves you all. I wish I could take every one of you to live with me. I'm just sorry that I can't." His eyes showed his hurt, his deep sadness. Then he left us alone with them. Our only strength and support just walked out the door. That's when I knew it was over.

"Mama, I can do more work around the house," Lee offered. "You won't have to work. I'll quit school and get a job."

"Lee, you're not old enough to quit school," Reverend Small chided him.

"Mama, I'd rather live with you, too," Richard said quietly.

"That's what I'd like, too, Richard. But I don't think it is going to work. I have to think of what's best for all of you. It's not just about me," Mama gently stated.

"Roy, come here." She patted the sofa beside her. Her voice was stern. I wobbled over on my spaghetti legs and stood, refusing to sit beside her.

"Roy, this is the hardest thing I've ever had to do. I've, we've tried to think of all the options. This is the best thing. You'll go to school there, you'll go to church, you'll have plenty of children to play with. You'll have good food to eat and clothes to wear. Besides, I know better than you, I haven't done a good job taking care of you this year. I can't even take care of myself sometimes."

"What about Lizzie and Tommy? Are they going, too?" Mary asked in a controlled voice. She'd regained her composure and demanded answers.

"No. They'll stay with me." Mama's answer was blunt. No details. Nothing else. Did I detect resentment or dishonesty or both?

"If you can't take care of us, how can you take care of them? They are the ones who need the most care," Mary stated with persistence. She made a lot of sense.

Mama looked at Reverend Small. He shrugged slightly. "I think I can handle taking care of those two until I can do something different. Besides, I'm hoping this is temporary."

"Like what?" I asked.

"Like getting a babysitter or putting them in a nursery. Don't worry about them."

"Daddy told me we had enough saved to take care of us."

"When did he tell you that?" Mama asked.

"The last time I saw him. In the sanitarium. Daddy knew he was dying. He knew it. He told me he'd saved money; the house was paid for, and he wanted us to always stay together. That's what he wanted." Mary was defiant. Admiration for my sister was growing by leaps and bounds.

"I'm sure that's what he told you, Mary," Mama agreed. "When he told you that, he probably meant it at the time. Remember, your daddy was very sick. He wasn't thinking right.

He left a lot of bills behind. The good church people have helped us, but we can't continue accepting their charity forever. The Lodge members have been good, but we can't continue accepting their handouts, either. I do have some pride left."

"So do we," Mary argued. "No other kids I know were ever given away."

That remark must have hit her hard. Mama straightened her shoulders and calmly said, "Well, that may be. Anyway, this is something that Reverend Small and the church elders have helped me with. They helped me find this place. It's somewhere that you can grow up in a healthy environment, where you can have three meals a day, where you can go to school and to church, and where you can become somebody when you're grown. We're the adults and we know what's best. I'm sorry this is my decision, but it is. You'll have to accept it."

I felt discarded. No good. I didn't matter to anyone.

"Your mother's right," Reverend Small said in his whiny, matter-of-fact voice. "We've all prayed a lot about this. And it is a sacrifice your mother is making—a huge sacrifice. She is making this decsion out of her love for you. You have to try and believe that. Besides, we believe you'll learn to like your new home."

"One more question, then. Does Mark know about this?" Mary asked.

"No, not yet," Mama replied. "I'll let him know, and I'll tell him where to write to you."

"When do we leave?" Lee asked.

"In a few days," Mama answered simply.

"So that's why you took us to see the doctor. That's why we had to have physicals and x-rays. Right?" Everything started falling into place now. "That why we've not been allowed to get the mail. That's why Reverend Small stays here more than he does at his own house. Right?" I asked.

"Roy! Watch your tone. And yes. It seems you've figured it all out." She was angry. After taking a deep breath, she continued in a calmer voice." You had to have complete check-ups and x-rays to make sure you didn't have T.B. and to make sure you were healthy."

"Do we have T.B.?" Richard timidly asked.

Mama smiled into his sweet, upturned face that was wet with tears. "No, son, you don't, thank God. You're healthy. And Roy, I have been writing to the orphanage and they've been writing to me. I didn't want to upset you until I knew what I was going to do. Reverend Small, can you show them their new home?" Mama asked.

He pulled out a black and white printed brochure from his lapel pocket. "It's rated as the number two orphanage in the country. It is a wonderful home for children, located close to Charlotte. That's close to the mountains. Every summer, all the kids go to camp for a week. The school is on the campus and has grades one through twelve. They have an infirmary in case you get sick, a wonderful Presbyterian church, a well-stocked library, peach orchards, apple orchards, a dairy farm, a vegetable garden, and so much more. I know the Superintendent in charge. His name is Superintendent Jackson. He's a good man—a very devout Christian. He has a family of his own who lives on the campus. He has a reputation for being kind, fair, and for running an orderly facility. I'm told the children really love and respect him."

Lee and Richard listened to his sales pitch. How easily swayed they were! Mary just stared at the floor, still, like a marble statue. I felt like that - cold, lifeless. Mama was listening, too. I'm sure she'd heard all of this before—from Reverend Small.

Later, when he was leaving, he instructed us. "I'll be taking you to the orphanage on Tuesday morning. Pack your best clothes and favorite toys. It's a long drive, so I'll be here around 7:30. Well, goodnight. Goodnight Iris."

"Goodnight and thank you again. Roy, go with Mary to get Lizzie and Tommy. And don't tell Mrs. Johnson or the children anything. Hear me?" Mama cautioned us.

"Mama is putting us in an orphanage." Mary started crying the minute Mrs. Johnson opened the door.

"What?" Mrs. Johnson gasped and tried to hide her astonishment. She covered her mouth with a wrinkled hand. "Oh, dear God, no! No! " She kept mumbling. "You poor children! You poor, poor children! What you have gone through."

"Mama told you not to say anything," I whispered to Mary.

"What's she gonna do to us now, Roy? Put us in an orphanage?"

Mary was right!

"We were told not to tell you anything, Mrs. Johnson. Promise you won't say anything to anybody," Mary pleaded. "We have to get home or she'll be mad. Thanks for taking care of the kids."

"I understand. I'll try not to say a word to anyone, but I will pray about this," she said. Mrs. Johnson gently bent to lift Tommy from a pallet on the floor. Mary took him from her. "Here's his little bottle. He didn't drink too much. He'd rather play than eat," Mrs. johnson said with a smile. Her voice was shaky.

Lizzie, who was sleepy, started crying on the way home. "Roy, it's spooky in the dark," she whimpered while dragging a naked doll by the arm.

"Hush, Lizzie. Nothin's gonna bother you. Then it dawned on me. We wouldn't be with Lizzie much longer. I snatched her up into my arms and hugged her so hard I easily could have cracked her tiny ribs.

"Lizzie, Lizzie. What will I do without you and Tommy?" My tears dripped on her yellow, cookie-smudged dress. I couldn't stop crying. I breathed deeply, so I could remember her smell forever.

"Roy," she pouted, struggling to be free. "Roy, you're hurtin me."

I hugged her hard just once more and placed her bare feet in the middle of the dirt street. She had a puzzled look on her tiny face, the little face I'd miss. It's funny. Until that moment - standing in the middle of Mercy Avenue under twinkling stars - I never realized how much I would miss my precious little sister.

"You all right, Pop?" Mary asked.

"Yeah. I'm all right."

"Well, we guessed it, didn't we?" she asked.

"Yeah, but it doesn't make it any easier, does it?"

"No. I still can't believe it's happening to us," she said in a low voice.

"Well it is. Know what, though?"

"What?" she asked.

"I think I can handle it as long as we're together. You're a fighter."

Mary shrugged and smiled. I could tell she was touched by my sincerity. We walked the rest of the way home in silence.

Chapter 34

It is God who arms me with strength and makes my way perfect.
"--Psalm 18:32"

Richard: The four of us sat resigned, quiet, motionless in the living room until our silence was broken by the car's motor. Mama had fixed us a big breakfast of grits, eggs, sausage, toast, and jelly. How ironic that she fixed breakfast for us on our last day home. Sort of like a prisoner's last meal before execution. We even had orange juice and milk, but the food, juice, and milk were wasted. We weren't hungry and hadn't been for several days. Mama stayed busy cooking and waiting on us. She kept her eyes diverted from ours and drank a cup of coffee leaning over the sink with her back to us.

Four suitcases held all the clothes and a few toys and trinkets we could pack. Mary wore a brown polka-dotted dress and white anklet socks and polished black shoes. Lee, Roy, and I were dressed in our Sunday clothes: long-sleeve white shirts, creased dark trousers, white socks, and polished black shoes. Lee wore Daddy's lapel pin in his collar. Roy stuffed his swimming medals in the zippered pouch of my suitcase because he didn't have any more room in his. Mary had placed Daddy's Bible in her suitcase. I held Lizzie and the wooden treasure box in my small lap and stroked her hair awkwardly, trying to mimic the adults I'd watched.

"Where y'all goin?" Lizzie kept asking. "Why ya dressed up? Kin I go, too?"

Mary busied herself dressing one of Lizzie's dolls. No one could explain this inconceivable thing to us, much less to her. Tommy slept in his crib with his favorite stuffed animal clutched tightly in one tiny hand. I wondered if Tommy would remember us? I wondered if we'd ever come back to visit this house on Mercy Avenue? Would we ever come back to live here? I wondered if Mama would come to visit us?

Uncle Bob came by while we tried to eat the breakfast.

He told us our other aunts and uncles loved us and would come to visit. They thought it would be easier for us if they didn't come to say good-bye in person, but they promised to write us letters.

"Mama's really upset about this. She can't believe you're doing it, Iris." I heard him whisper to Mama.

Mama just drummed her fingers on the arms of Daddy's chair. Her eyes were focused on the curtains above our heads. I thought it was strange she couldn't look at us or talk to us before we left. Uncle Bob heard the car's motor when we did. He gave Mama a questioning look that seemed to ask, "Iris, are you really sure about this?" No one was going to change her mind. Not now.

She rose slowly from her chair and started to the door. I thought she was going to fall. It seemed like her knees just buckled.

"Mama!" I cried!

Uncle Bob caught her arm.

"I'm okay, Richard," she smiled. "Thanks."

Mama grabbed Lee and hugged him tightly. The dam' broke and started an avalanche of tears. She gently stroked my hair and kissed me on the forehead. My eyes were blurred with tears, so I couldn't see her face. It looked like she was smiling.

"I love you, Mama," I said. "Don't worry about us. We'll be all right."

"I know you will. I know you will." She cried and rubbed my fingers, my arms, my shoulders, as if touching the parts of my body would help her remember me.

"Mommie? Mommie? Stop cryin!" Lizzie whined. She stamped her tiny feet, demanding the attention she wasn't getting.

Mama finally let me go and moved on to Mary. She kissed her softly on the cheek and whispered, "I do love you. I hope you can understand, someday. Don't let them forget that I love them."

Then, she stood in front of Roy. "I know you hate me right now, and you don't understand why this is happening, but some day you will. Roy, I pray that you will understand. You'll have to try and forgive me. I love you. I always have." When she reached for Roy, he dodged her.

"Right." He picked up his bag and steadily walked out the door and climbed into the black Plymouth. We followed him and placed our suitcases in the awaiting trunk that was ready to swallow up our meager belongings. Following Roy would become our norm.

Roy sat in the backseat between Lee and me. Mary sat in the front beside Reverend Small.

"Don't worry, Iris. I'll let you know when we get there." He took Mama's hand and extended his hand to shake Uncle Bob's, but Uncle Bob declined.

Uncle Bob raised his right hand and waved to us. Lizzie was standing beside Mama with her thumb in her mouth.

"Bye-bye," she cried and waved. "Bye-bye." Her baby doll lay abandoned on the porch beside her bare feet. When would we ever see her again?

Reverend Small cranked the car and eased it backwards. The car crept slowly down the street. Russell Thomas stood on his front porch without his normal smirk. He just watched as we passed by. When we were almost beyond his house, he raised his hand to say good-bye. Roy returned the wave with a smile to his favorite nemesis. Somehow, I guess the word had gotten out.

I saw the oak tree off to the right. I'd never forget how special that weedy place had been to us – to me.

"Look, Richard! Look! It's Mrs. Johnson!" Lee cried.

She beckoned the Reverend to stop his car. Slowly, he did.

"Good morning, Reverend Small."

"Good morning, Mrs. Johnson. How have you been?"

"I've been better, if you know what I mean. Forgive me, Reverend, but I wanted to say good-bye to the children and to give them some cookies for the trip." She leaned into the open window on my side of the car. "Good-bye, darlings. I will miss all of you, and I'll pray for each of you every night. Don't forget me, ever. Write to me, and I'll write you back." Her loving eyes were flooded with tears. I watched them spill down her lightly-rouged cheeks, making little white paths that traveled down her face. "Don't forget me. I love all of you." She briefly touched my face. Then she walked quickly inside her house. We watched her go, choking down the lumps in our throats. Then Reverend Small eased the car forward again. I turned my head to look out the window and began crying softly.

"Stop the car! Stop the car!" Roy screamed.

Reverend Small slammed on the brakes.

"Wh-what's wrong?" He shouted.

"Mary, open the door." Roy cried. "Hurry." He shoved the front seat and Mary forward. She almost hit her head on the dashboard. He climbed over Lee and ran down the street. I'd never seen him run that fast. We turned to see Roy jumping over two steps at a time to land on the front porch where Mama was still standing.

He threw his arms around her waist and just stayed in that position. Reverend Small backed the car down the road and stopped in front of our house.

"Mama, I do love you. I do love you," we heard him say. "And I want you to love me, too."

"I do love you, Roy. I do love you more than you can ever know. One day you'll understand just how much."

Uncle Bob was crying as he looked on. It was hard to see our grown uncle cry. Roy and Mama held each other for a long time. Then, Roy let go of Mama and ran down the steps for the last time. He climbed into the backseat between Lee and me and stared forward. He was ready, and his courage was contagious for all of us.

We stopped briefly at the stop sign where Roy used to meet Daddy every day. I knew he had to be remembering those times. Reverend Small carefully glanced in both directions and turned the car to the right.

Mechanically, all of us (except Roy) turned to look behind us one more time. I silently hoped for a miracle. Maybe Mama would be running down the road after the car and shouting, "Stop! I've changed my mind!"

But when I looked back, the only thing I saw were the framed houses lining the dirt street. The street we'd known and loved and called ours. The street where we had called home - until now. I turned in my seat to look ahead. We had no idea what this new place would be like, but it was where we were headed. It would become our new home, and Daddy and Granny would be hovering close by.

Chapter 35

Never bend your head. Always hold it high. Look the world straight in the eye.
Helen Keller

Roy: Not even the ugly red stop sign could stop us this time. In the end, it was strange to realize this authoritative sign that had defined our boundaries and our lives for so long was nothing more than a piece of wood and thin metal. Its authority stopped at the end of the road. That's all, nothing more.

We counted electric poles and other black cars on the two-lane road that carried us from the eastern part of North Carolina west to the central part of the state. We painfully listened to the monotone monologue of our driver until he finally realized he was talking to himself. So after stopping for a bathroom break and Cokes that he paid for, we continued the long, warm trip in silence except for the static of the radio. He found a gospel music station that lasted for a town or two without the irritating static. Then, after seven miserable hours, we had our first glimpses of "home."

"Here we are children. Finally here. Look! What do you think? This is your new home!" He announced joyfully. I'm sure he was as happy to get rid of us as we were to get rid of him.

The campus was massive with lots of big buildings laid out on both sides of the two-lane road. There were peach and apple orchards as far as you could see on either side. Real cows and real goats – not pictures like we were used to - grazed in the green grassy meadows. Children of all ages walked, ran, or skipped everywhere. They were all smiling and laughing. I don't know what I expected to see. Maybe I expected a bunch of sad, skinny little kids with torn clothes. That's not what I was seeing.

I looked at Richard. His eyes were wide.

"What do ya think, Richard?" I whispered.

"I've dreamed about this place, Pop. This is the place I dreamed about. I think we're gonna be okay."

I didn't question him. I looked at Lee who was staring at a bunch of girls. They waved and giggled as we rode by. He waved back and grinned. I couldn't see Mary's face, but I noticed her head was like mine, turning back and forth. I guess she was taking in all of the sights, making her initial judgements. At long last, we turned into a lengthy graveled driveway and stopped in front of a two-story brick building with black shutters and lots of blind-covered windows. The huge porch had white columns.

"Okay, children. End of the trip. We're here. This is the Administration Building where Superintendent Jackson works. Let's go in, and I'll introduce you." He seemed relieved.

Before we could climb out of the backseat of the car, a tall man with gentle blue eyes and a big, genuine-looking smile strode out onto the porch of the huge building. His brown hair was parted on the left and combed neatly to the side. He wore brown tweed suit pants, a white shirt with the sleeves rolled up at his elbows, and a dark brown tie. He looked to be around 40, maybe 45.

"Hello, Reverend Small. I'm glad you had a safe trip." They shook hands, then he stuck his hands into his pants pockets.

"Hello! Superintendent Jackson. So good to see you again! It's been a long time? How have you been?"

"Fine, just fine. We can catch up later. I hope you can stay a little while."

"Sure. A little while. I'd like to get home by midnight. It's takes a little more than seven hours."

"Good." He turned his full attention to us. "I'd like to meet these young folks, now. You must be Mary," he smiled and extended his hand to shake hers. Welcome to your new home. I hope you're going to like it here, Mary. We're happy to have you join our family."

"Thank you, sir," Mary said and returned his smile.

Lee climbed out of the backseat ahead of Richard and me.

"Let's see. You're the tall one, so that means you must be Lee. Right? I heard you were a charmer and indeed you are. Welcome to your new home, Lee. We have lots of things to do. I think you'll like it here." He patted Lee on the back.

Lee grinned, "Thanks." Then he shyly glanced around and started shifting his weight from leg to leg.

"And you must be little Richard?"

"Yes, sir." Richard shook his hand like a grown up.

"Welcome Richard. This is your new home. I've heard that you especially enjoy going to church and reading your Bible. Our church here is called Little Joe's. It's named after a little boy who used to live here. He raised money to build the church. Remind me to tell you the story about Little Joe once you get settled in. Okay?" he asked.

"Okay," Richard said. When he grinned, his dimples appeared. This was one of those times. "But right now, I need to go to the bathroom."

"Okay. Walk inside the door there and ask Miss Ashley if she'll show you where it is."

After Richard disappeared inside the building, the tall man walked over to me. "So by process of elimination, that means you have to be Roy. Right?" He asked.

"Yes, sir."

"Well, Roy. Welcome to your new home. I hear you're quite the competitor. We have lots of sports activities here, so you should enjoy playing on the basketball team, the baseball team, and the football team. Here, you become part of a bigger, more diverse family. You'll have lots of boys and girls to play with and compete with. I hope you'll like it here, too, Roy."

"I hope so. I just don't know, but I'll give it a try." I didn't know what else to say. His eyes held mine. It was like he was trying to read my mind.

"That's an honest answer. I like that. Say, isn't your nickname Pop?"

"Yes, sir."

"Where did you get that nickname, Roy?"

"From Pop Warner. Football is my favorite sport. Pop Warner was one of the greatest college football coaches ever. He's my hero. Everyone knows that, so that's how I got the nickname." I was happy to talk about football anytime.

"I should have guessed. Well, that's a good nickname for you, Roy. I'm going to do everything I can to make you and your family happy here."

With that, he extended his large hand and took mine in his own. His firm grasp conveyed honesty, strength, sincerity, safety. Somehow, I felt okay, like everything was going to be fine. And I felt something else that was kind of weird. I felt like I already knew him and he already knew me. He'd made us feel welcome by taking the time to know something about us, by meeting us at the door, and by calling us each by name. We finally belonged somewhere and someone cared about us. In my heart, I believed him and knew he was a man who meant what he said and said what he meant. He was a man I could possibly trust - again.

Chapter 36

Take time to be friendly — It is the road to happiness.
Take time to dream – It is hitching your wagon to a star.
Take time to love and to be loved – It is the privilege of the gods.
Take time to look around – It is too short a day to be selfish.
Take time to laugh – It is the music of the soul.
Old English Prayer

Roy: The metal ashtray was full of cigarette butts as Roy snubbed the remainder of his last Winston. Absentmindedly, he drummed the silver lighter on the scarred table.

Tommy sat silently, watching his brother's monotonous movements. He turned sideways in his chair and stretched his long legs.

"Pop, when was that?" Tommy asked.

"We entered the home in November 1941."

"And Lizzie?"

"Christmas Eve, 1941. The bombing of Pearl Harbor wasn't enough. Mama sent another bomb," Roy smirked.

"I don't follow."

"We all thought she'd keep you and Lizzie and not send you to the home with us. At least, we were hoping that you two would grow up in the house on Mercy Avenue. I guess we still believed in a Norman Rockwell life for you and Lizzie. We were both shocked and happy to see her standing beside the big Christmas tree in Rumple Hall on Christmas Eve. We'd really been homesick, and she was a happy reminder of home. It was like a small family reunion. Richard. Well of course, he was the happiest to see her. After all, he'd always been the one to take care of her and play with her. So, Lizzie was our Christmas present that year."

"So I came just a few months later, right? I guess she'd gotten tired of me, too, by then." Tommy said with a sigh.

"Naw. I don't know." Roy shrugged. "From what we understood, she did try to keep you. By then, she'd gotten a job working at a soda fountain in a nearby drugstore. Grandma kept you during the day while she worked. The story goes she didn't make enough money and didn't have the time or stamina to take care of you at night. So, you showed up three months later, out of the clear blue without any warning. Just like Lizzie."

"I don't remember," stated Tommy.

"I'm not surprised. You were just about two."

"You fellas want another drink or something else to eat?" The waitress broke their silence. "With all the talking you've been doing, I'm surprised you're not parched."

"Yeah, bring us another one," Roy replied. "Got any cigarettes?"

"Yeah, there's a machine in the back."

"Good. Tommy, I'll be right back." Roy limped down the narrow aisle towards the back of the restaurant. Tommy heard a jingle and then something dropping. Then he heard Roy's returning footsteps.

"Well, at least we were altogether," Tommy said breaking the silence.

Roy peeled the cellophane off the top of the pack of cigarettes and tore an opening. He patted the bottom of the pack and gingerly pulled an extending cigarette out of the package.

"Yeah, I guess you could say that. For a while we were, but the place was so big – 300 kids or more. And we were all divided up, living in different buildings."

"Weren't you and Lee together most of the time?"

"Yeah. When we first got there, Mary went to live in one of the girls' buildings. I don't remember which one. Lee and I were placed in Lee's Cottage. Richard went to Synod. As we got older, we all made the normal progression through the buildings, just like you. What was it? Synod, Lees, Jennie Gilmer, Quads?"

"Yeah, but don't forget Baby Cottage. That's where I went first. Lizzie, too."

The waitress interrupted them. "Here ya are fellows! Two ice cold drinks. Anything else?"

"No, thanks." Tommy winked. "But keep an eye on us. You never know." They both laughed.

"You're something!" She said rolling her eyes. When she strolled away slowly to wait on another couple, Tommy turned back to Roy.

"Hey Pop! Remember the good old truck farm? Picking peaches in the orchard? Did you work at the dairy?"

"No, but Lee and Richard did. I got out of that fun by working at the print shop."

They both laughed.

"I think the worst thing we had to do was having to take baths with other boys in the same bathtub," Roy added.

"Me too. I totally agree. We had to do that for how long?" Tommy asked.

"I can't remember, but I hated having to get in cold, dirty bath water that other boys had just gotten out of. I hated that."

"Yeah. I remember that, too. But by the time you got to the Quads, you could take showers – alone!" He laughed.

"Yeah. You're right."

They each drank swallows of Coke© from the cold glass bottles and grew quiet. "And the food was pretty good, I thought," Tommy offered.

"Did you really think so?" Roy asked incredulously.

"Yeah. I don't recall ever being hungry. We had plenty of fruits and vegetables. Chicken on Sundays. Grits, molasses. Sometimes cookies and cakes when the Presbyterian women brought them for us."

"No sugar during World War II. I remember that," Roy added.

"Well anyway, the food wasn't that bad."

"No. You're right. It wasn't."

"Do you remember going to the movies?" asked Tommy.

"Sure. I'd work odd jobs to earn enough money so I could go every Saturday. Once in a while, people donated tickets, so we got to go free."

"Didn't you have to be 13?"

"Yeah. You couldn't go to the movies on your own until you were 13. But you got to go in groups when you were younger. I remember seeing *Gone with the Wind* and *The Wizard of Oz*. I thought they were something special – in color and on the big screen." Roy laughed. "The first time I went, I ate so much candy, I got sick on the way home and threw up."

Tommy joined in his laughter. "You know what? I remember when Richard used to go to the movies on Saturday nights with a group. I'd find him waiting for me on the church steps before Sunday School. He'd give me a piece of candy and tell me not to tell any of the other kids cause he'd brought it back especially for me. He didn't have any more to share and didn't want to hurt anyone's feelings."

"Really?" Roy asked with a smile. "I never knew he did that."

"Yeah. He always brought candy back and shared it with me. Lizzie, too, I think. He felt sorry for us since we weren't old enough to go yet. He was real considerate."

"Yes, he was at that," Roy agreed.

Tommy took another long swallow of his drink. He quietly placed the bottle on the table.

"You know. I remember going to his funeral, but that's about all. I can't remember much more."

Roy signed heavily and shook his head. "He had just celebrated his thirteenth birthday on the twenty-fifth. He was excited about becoming a teenager," Roy paused, took a draw of his cigarette and continued. "They said it was the quickest case of meningitis they'd ever seen. He'd gotten up that morning complaining of an earache, so they sent him to the Infirmary. They dressed his ear and sent him back to the Quad to lie down. But it didn't get any better. It got worse. Then his head began hurting really bad. His roommate, Patrick, said he was crying because the pain was so bad. Patrick convinced him to go back to the Infirmary, but when he tried to stand up, he just fell down. He asked Patrick to carry him, and Patrick did. Think about it. A 13 year-old carrying another 13 year-old across the road to the Infirmary. They checked him and immediately called an ambulance to take him to Statesville. His fever was already high, and he was in a lot of pain. They say he lasted only a few hours."

They were silent for a few minutes.

"I don't think I've ever had a death hit me so hard. It hit everyone hard. I couldn't believe all the flowers that were sent from people all over the community. Richard was a popular boy, and everyone loved him," Roy said with a smile. "You know, Tommy, when Richard died, a part of all of us died with him. He was really, really special. I miss him a lot."

"I still don't understand why she didn't come to the funeral."

"Me neither. It was bad enough that she didn't come to visit us while we were there…."

Tommy interrupted. "Well, I can't say that because she did start visiting Lizzie and me after you, Mary, and Lee were gone."

"Yeah. To be fair, she did. But for the six years we were there, we didn't hear a word from her. Mark's letters were the only way we kept up with him or Mama. And at least, Mark did visit us. Just like all the aunts and uncles. Some came more, some came only once, but at least they came."

"When did you leave?"

"June 19, 1947. Richard was buried on June 6. With Mary just graduating and going to live with Aunt Jeannie, there was no way I was going to stay there any longer."

"What about Lee?"

"Lee had gotten use to the place. He had lots of friends, lots of girlfriends, and by then, we traveled in different crowds, had different interests. I knew he'd be fine. You and Lizzie, too. Besides, it was the only home either of you knew

– or could remember."

"When Uncle Thomas and Aunt Susan came to the funeral, they offered me a place to live and a job working with him at the bottling plant. I wasn't about to pass that offer up. It was heaven to my ears, and it turned out okay. I was much happier."

Tommy looked away, then down. "Pop, I've never told anyone this, but I saw Richard once."

"What do you mean?" Roy asked.

"After he died. I saw him. I know you won't believe me, but it's true. Scout's honor."

"You were never a Scout," Roy reminded him.

"I know. But I was a Marine," he laughed.

"Yep. That's true."

"Anyway, one night in Jennie Gilmer Cottage, I was almost asleep when I noticed a young boy standing beside a chest-of-drawers across from my bed. He looked a little older than me, and I remember wondering why this kid was out of bed and dressed when it was so late. This kid had dark hair and was wearing a white shirt and dark shorts. I didn't want him to get into any trouble, so I asked him if he was lost. All he did was just stand there in the shadows and smile at me. He didn't say anything. I turned over to see if my roommate was asleep. I wanted to know if he knew who this kid was. When I looked back, he was gone. He'd just vanished into nowhere."

Roy silently stared at his cigarette lighter.

"I knew it. You don't believe me, do you?"

Roy waited a few minutes. "Actually, I do believe you. I believe in visions and stuff like that. And if it was Richard, then he came back to make sure you were okay."

"Why me, Pop?"

"Cause. That was just the way Richard was. He cared about everybody. And besides, you just described what he was wearing the night he died."

"You're kidding?"

"Nope. I'm not. Scout's honor." They laughed.

"I believe Richard had a gift that was unique. He found the key to life at an early age, and he shared it with everyone he knew," Roy paused and sighed. "Wanna know what else he was wearing when he died?"

"Yeah, sure," Tommy replied. "What?"

"He was wearing a string around his neck. On the string was a key."

"A key? What kind of key?"

"It was the key to Mercy Avenue—Daddy's house key. You see, Richard always believed that we'd go home again some day. He never gave up hope that Mama would come and get us and take us back home again. He used to reminisce about playing marbles under the house and hide-n-seek in the dark. He talked about the days when we played horsey and jockey." Roy's eyes were misty and had a far-away look. "Know what else? I like to think he did go home again. I just have to believe that he did, and when he got there, he was able to use that little key on the string he kept around his neck all those years."

He cleared his throat and continued with a smile on his face. "Yeah, and when he got there, he used his key – Richard's Key."

Epilogue

As for man, his days are like grass, he flourishes like a flower of the field: the wind blows over it and it is gone, and its place remembers it no more. But from everlasting to everlasting the Lord's love is with those who fear him, and his righteousness with their children's children – with those who keep his covenant and remember to obey his precepts.
Psalm 103: 15–18

Richard: On June 6, 1947, I wore the biggest smile ever on my face as I stood between two people that I dearly loved. We held each other's hands and watched family members and close friends gathered around a tiny grave, now filled in and covered with lovely bouquets of summer flowers, wreaths of delicate red roses, and sprays of gladiolas mingled with baby's breath. I picked up a single red rose and held it to my nose to breathe in its heavenly fragrance. After a few moments, we turned away from the mourners. Almost instantly, we were walking down a well-known street.

"Wait," I said. "Please wait just a minute. I need to stop."

They obliged me.

I walked over to a dark car that was parked beside a red stop sign. The pretty lady inside was sobbing bitterly, and I pitied her. I wanted to wrap my arms around her and tell her not to cry. I wanted to assure her that everything was all right. I wanted to tell her that she had been forgiven. I wanted to touch her hair and kiss her face one last time. But I couldn't; not just yet. Instead, I tenderly placed the rose on her lap and backed away. I returned to my patient and silent partners who were accompanying me on this special journey.

Then we continued past the red stop sign and began traveling along a narrow path that led to the the loving arms that were spread wide to welcome us and embrace us with eternal peace.

About This Book

My heart was pounding in my chest and my breath was coming rapidly. Public speaking, polled as the number one most frightening thing by adults, was not my forte, either. Take a deep breath, and exhale slowly I reminded myself.

When the phone rang several weeks earlier and a church friend asked me to deliver a special offering message on this Sunday before Thanksgiving, I readily agreed because I had an invested interest and sentimental reasons for agreeing to deliver this small message. The special offering would go to a children's home in our locale.

When the minister introduced me, I took another deep breath, walked to the front of the church, and began speaking.

"In 1941, four brothers and two sisters—ages 2 to 13— were uprooted from their home in Wilmington, North Carolina and moved to a Presbyterian orphanage which is now a Children's Home. The eldest boy of this group was my father."

By now, breathing was coming at a regular more normal pace. My voice was getting louder as I spoke each word, and the tone of my voice carried confidence and sincerity. I looked out into the sea of faces and read peaked interests in their various countenances. They thought this would be one of the normal solicitation messages for special offerings. I would not let this be an ordinary one.

"My father never romanticized about his childhood or his past. The few details we stole from him were answers to squelch our thirsty questions to learn more about life in an orphanage. He spoke briefly about working on the farm to grow crops, going to school, going to church and learning the Catechisms, and singing in a choir. Excitement crept into his baritone voice as he recalled playing on the football team. As we opened our many gifts from Santa Claus, he watched and smiled with glee. Then, as the day wore on and we tired of our new treasures, he would get this far-away look in his brown eyes. Then, he would speak of his childhood Christmases there and how each child was permitted to write to Santa asking for one toy. His first year there, he asked for a football, but instead he received a basketball. His following year there, he asked for the football again, but he received a soccer ball. It is questionable to me if he ever received a football during his tenure at the orphanage."

Sympathetic, audible laughter and mouth-covered chuckles broke the intensity of the moment. I was relieved because my emotions were starting to get the best of me. In the back of my mind, I recalled my public speaking training— good eye contact, emphasis on special words, pauses, humor, sincerity, and a true interest in what you are speaking about —among a few.

"Another alumnus of the orphanage that I spoke with reminisced that all she ever wanted was a raincoat of her very own. After asking for it for seven years, she finally received it when she was a junior in high school. It became a priceless treasure to her."

"My daddy taught me that we all should be thankful for what we have whether it's a lot or a little. It was my father who introduced me to church services and took me to Sunday School and Worship throughout my early childhood years. My mother and sister would join us in my later childhood and teen years. The orphanage instilled four basic values in its children, and my daddy lived them well. In turn, he passed these four values onto my sister and me. Before I tell you about these four values, let me give you a little history lesson."

"This Synodical Orphanage was originally founded in 1891 as a Presbyterian arm of the Church to meet the needs of the least of God's children. 'The children were to labor daily at domestic employments, gardening, agricultural labor or mechanical pursuits.' It was specifically founded 'to prepare helpless orphan children of our church for good citizenship and to lead useful lives."

"Today, as a Children's Home, it continues to meet the needs of children and families who are desperate for help in the name of Christ and in the name of God's Church. The kids who come to the Home today have academic, social, emotional, or behavioral problems. Some have attempted suicide several times.

Most have been physically, emotionally, or sexually abused. The Home's goal is to reunite families. Incumbent's ages are from ten to 21 years old. An average stay is around nine months but can be anywhere from two weeks to four years or more. Children stay until their needs are met. Thirty percent do not have an environment to which they can return. Therapeutic counseling is provided, whether it be pyschological, psychiatric, special education, or social counseling to both the children and their parents."

"The Home has always had four core values which were, and still are, the establishment of 1) sound Christian nurture, 2) academic preparation , 3) work ethics, and 4) funfilled recreation." I was on a roll now and could have spoken forever, or at least until my notes were exhausted.

"My father left the orphanage in June 1947. With his departure, he left behind three brothers and one sister-three to complete their remaining years of childhood and education and one to begin his eternal life with God. Almost six years after their arrival and just ten days after celebrating his thirteenth birthday, one of the younger brothers whose goal was to become a minister, complained of a terrible headache after attending morning worship services. He was literally carried by his thirteen year-old roommate, a dear member of our church, to the orphanage's infirmary. By one o'clock the next morning, he was pronounced dead, a victim of spinal meningitis. This young boy whose life ended so abruptly is buried at the present Presbyterian Church's cemetery located on the orphanage's campus. His small grave is marked by a modest square stone that bears only his name, his date of birth, and his date of death. There is no epitaph etched in the stone or no ornamentation. He was born simply in a city whose motto is 'persevere.' He lived simply, died simply, but with that elegant simplicity, he left behind a legacy of endearing love and care for others."

"Finally, while researching for a book I hope to write one day, I ran across the vast lists of contributors of food, clothes, toys, and money throughout the orphanage's history. Among them was the name of this church, my church. You have been a part of my heritage before I ever knew it. So, from the bottom of my heart, I personally want to say thank you for all your generosity shown to my family and other orphans in the past. Today, this is a Children's Home. I beseech you to continue helping in this worthwhile cause. If we want to help save lives and change the future, then this is a worthy place to start."

I knew when I returned to my pew, the hearts and ears of many had been touched. The special offering collected for the Home was tripled the amount normally collected in the past. My heart had spoken directly to others' hearts that day. Never underestimate the compassion of the human heart. I cannot help but to recall what the Bible says in James 1:27 (NIV):

Religion that God our Father accepts as pure and faultless is this: to look after orphans and widows in their distress and to keep oneself from being polluted by the world.

One of our church's Cub Scout Leaders telephoned me that Sunday afternoon and asked me to give the same "talk" to the Cub Scouts and their parents. Their mission that Christmas was to help the same Children's Home with donations of needed items.

On the following Monday night, I delivered the same "talk" to the parents and Scouts. My husband and I volunteered to take the donations to the Children's Home which was twenty five miles from the church. After a week's worth of collections, their responses in donated items were phenomenal. My heart was touched. Among the items were toiletries, books, socks, clothes, underwear, shoes, school supplies, stationery, envelopes, and toys. Tears sprang to my eyes when I noticed three footballs sitting on top of the boxes of toys.

The Scout Leaders and other parents helped load the carefully packed cardboard boxes into the back of my husband's white work van. We thanked everyone, they thanked us, and we were on our way to the Children's Home. Along the way, it began snowing. The blustering, large flakes pounded the windshield of our vehicle severely effecting the visibility ahead as we found our way through the sparsely-populated backroads. The night's darkness seemed eerie and uncommon. The flakes appeared to come at us rather than around us. We looked at each other and smiled. It was pretty; we were not worried. According to the weather report, there was no threat of accumulation or treacherous sleet or ice - just a beautiful gift of snow in the midst of a pre-winter's night.

My gaze fixed beyond the headlights of our vehicle now penetrating the beauty of this night to a time 56 years before when four little children were traveling these same backroads to a new home. Their pilgrimage to this unknown place had taken place on a late autumn November day, not a pre-winter December night. One little child of the same family did arrive on a Christmas Eve night. I wondered what she must have been thinking about during her car ride? What were she leaving behind? What was ahead for her? Would she ever return to her home? Who would befriend her? Who would nurture her? Who would love her?

Thus, began my pilgrimage into the writing of this book. In the years of my childhood, my father, aunts, and uncles spoke affectionately of the brother they left behind. He had wanted to become a minister when he grew up. Even though his dream seemed never fulfilled, through the research and conversations with family and acquaintances who knew Richard, the realization dawned on me that while he was here on earth for even a short while, he did in fact minister to those who loved him and knew him best. He touched the lives of many, leaving behind him kindness, virtue, love and treasured memories. Several of my cousins lovingly bare his name. While much of this book is fictionalized because of the scarcity of known facts about him, the loving memory of Richard continues to persevere in its pages.

About the Author

Sandi Huddleston-Edwards, author of the new novel *Richard's Key*, has a passion for writing. Even as a child, she spent her summer vacations in her bedroom reading and writing poems and short stories. Her favorite reads were *Little Women* and *Black Beauty*.

Sandi is a local talent and a native of North Carolina. Born in High Point, she grew up in Durham. Today she resides in Huntersville. After earning her A.A. degree from Central Piedmont Community College, she attended the University of North Carolina – Charlotte, where she earned her B.A. and M.A. degrees in English. As a life-long learner, she enjoys teaching others the art and science of writing by teaching part-time at CPCC and Montreat College. Her favorite classes to teach are English Composition and Professional Documentation.

While researching the paternal side of her family, Sandi was intrigued to learn more about a young uncle whose passionate goal in life was to become a minister. Even though he only lived 13 years, the way he lived his life and the way he inspired others was a story that deserved to be told; thus, this is the impetus for writing *Richard's Key*. It is a beautiful and poignant story of a faithful life and the lessons a young boy left behind.

When not pursuing her passions for writing and teaching, Sandi loves to travel, especially to Paris, Charleston, and San Francisco, "the three prettiest cities on the earth." In addition to spending time with her husband, hearing her son who is in seminary preach, and playing with her Yorkshire Terrier, she enjoys re-discovering the world through the eyes of her three grandchildren, Chase, Chesney, and Railey.